Worlds in Transition

Stories by Peter Dingus

Published by SpeculativeFictionReview.com

www.speculativefictionreview.com

Copyright © 2017 by Peter Dingus

ISBN 978-0-9785232-8-2

Cover art by Peter Dingus.

Worlds in
Transition

www.speculativefictionreview.com

To my loving family, Annie, John, and Paul.

Introduction

When you finally understand the universe, it will not only be stranger than you imagine, it will be stranger than you can imagine. – Arthur C. Clarke

The last hundred years has been a unique time in human history. The scientific advances of the twentieth century have been nothing short of breathtaking and have transformed much of the world in the process. But even the scientists that have created this new vision of the world have trouble understanding it intuitively.

When Einstein first introduced Special Relativity in 1905, the scientific community was dumfounded that someone could propose a theory in which different observers in uniform relative motion would be subject to time passing at different rates. Einstein was not talking about an illusion; he was describing a universe in which twins, depending on where they had been and how they had gotten there, would actually age differently. Most rational people found such a proposal to be ridiculous on its face.

But even Einstein found it hard to reconcile his intuition with another theory he helped create. Einstein held fast to a geometric vision of the universe that quantum mechanics violated by construction. As brilliant as he was, Einstein, with Boris Podolsky and Nathan Rosen, came up with the famous EPR Paradox in order to show that quantum mechanics couldn't possibly be right. In this scenario, two objects, quantum mechanically linked, somehow communicate the result of a measurement of one of them with the other, even though they are separated so as to prohibit any cause and effect relationship between them. The fact that quantum mechanics seems to supersede our common notions of cause and effect is the *paradox* part of EPR. The EPR Paradox was airtight and cleverly constructed to be both consistent with quantum mechanics, and inconsistent with common sense. Einstein felt confident that, in time, experiments would prove him right and that common sense would prevail.

When experiments were finally done, quantum mechanics was proven correct. To this day, most scientists will admit that they don't really understand the picture of the world that quantum mechanics paints.

Now we have string theory, with its pronouncements of a Multiverse (many universes that coexist simultaneously) and some seven new dimensions to our universe, which, to all appearances, seems three-dimensional. Though string theory is not an experimentally proven theory, like relativity and quantum mechanics, which are proven, it is nevertheless taken seriously by some of the world's greatest scientists.

So what are we to make of this new vision of the universe? I have personally gotten a sense of wonder and relevance actually seeing particles and anti-particles being spontaneously created and annihilated in high-energy particle detectors. Or, as in the work of my thesis, observing particles of light traveling through space and continuously changing into other particles of matter just long enough to escape the measurement of their masses. The reality of these things presents a unique portal into the true nature of our existence and the bizarre possibilities they would present if we were ever to come face to face with such truths. This, to me, is the essence of science fiction.

Worlds in Transition is a set of three stories that explore the human aspect of the mysteries of the new science. The book The Fabric of Reality, in part, inspired the first story, *The End of the World*. The author of The Fabric of Reality, David Deutsch, is one of the original proponents of quantum computers and is a well-known physicist and mathematician. The second story, *Parallax*, was born of a fascination with the Many Worlds interpretation of quantum mechanics, which was introduced in the late 1950's by Hugh Everett to try to explain quantum interference. In my opinion, the double slit interference pattern of single photons is a much more convincing argument for a Multiverse than is string theory. And finally, the third story, *One Way Ticket*, pays homage to relativity and string theory.

So at a time in history when competing beliefs centered on mystical, scientific, and spiritual views of the world clash as strongly as ever, it is up to you, dear reader, to determine whether I've succeeded in bringing to you my own personal *sense of wonder* at our new understanding of reality.

Peter Dingus, January 2017

Book One: The End of the World

In Memory of William Hargreaves and
Andy Hasenfeld.

The End of the World

I watched the coarse crimson sand seeping through the fingers of my gloved hands like the sand in an hourglass. Sparkles shone from small pieces of silicon crystals as they caught errant reflections from my helmet lights. There wasn't much else to do as I waited for the inevitable.

Off in the distance, over a fork shaped spire in the Kepler Range, I saw the odd object moving upward against the stationary field of similar bright points in the night sky. The Com, chirping in my ear, broke a thick silence.

"Liam?"

"Yeah."

"We've got the Comsat, come on in."

"Yeah, I see it," I said, unable to take my eyes off the orbiting star. I climbed to my feet from my rocky perch and started for the trailer. It was no more than a couple of hundred yards beyond the craggy rise in front of me, but I couldn't see it, didn't want to. I'd found this spot precisely for that reason. I wanted to be alone, but not so far away that I'd miss Mars-Geo when the Comsat was finally overhead again.

I gripped the rocks on either side of the cramped meandering path over the ridge as I climbed toward the ledge overlooking the trailer. I never took my eyes from the moving point of light slowly arcing across the sky. Once on top, I surveyed the mesa beyond the mountains on whose foothills I stood. The trailer was barely discernable from the dark ground around it. In the distance, I saw the golden suggestion of dawn, still an hour away behind the mountaintops to the east.

A short time later, I entered the main cabin airlock, removed my environment suit, and entered the cabin. Sanderson and Laird were focused on the large flat screen at the far end of the room, but Teresa turned as I clicked the airlock door shut.

"Liam," she said in a rushed whisper.

"Have I missed anything?"

"No, not really." She lowered her eyes. "The Comsat was unable to raise Pasadena; we just got a connection to Mission Control on SS Freedom."

"That bad?" I said carelessly, then regretted the slip.

"Uh-huh," she said, and turned back to the screen.

I didn't recall ever seeing the face on the monitor before, although by the distraught disheveled look of the man, even if I had known him, I might not have recognized him. His face filled the entire screen. The lighting was so bad that the resulting shadows made his drawn features look especially haggard. The skin under his red eyes was puffy and dark, making it look as if he'd been crying.

"At 6:15 A.M., Eastern Standard time, planetary defense targeting satellites identified several unidentified sub-orbital missiles coming over the North Pole from Kazakhstan," the man said. "Orbital defense platforms were unable to fire before offensive missiles deployed thousands of decoys. Roughly five missiles got through and destroyed large parts of Washington and New York."

He seemed to choke as if he were out of breath, then stared into the cabin for a few moments.

"Come on, come on," implored Sanderson, hoping as I did that it had all stopped there. Unfortunately, due to the hundred million miles that separated us from Space Station

Freedom orbiting the Earth, a two-way conversation was not possible, and we had to wait for the man to regain his composure on his own. When he started talking again, we learned it hadn't ended there, not by a long shot. With zombie-like persistence, the man continued to describe the fantastic events that, to the few of us left alive, signaled the end of our run on earth as a species. After the first strike there must have been total confusion and chaos, but the man seemed to acknowledge none of it. He continued to relate the facts concerning the end of the world as if he were reading from a well-vetted documentary script, like something that had happened to some lost race in the dim past, to which we had little emotional attachment. As he continued to speak, I heard low murmurs from Teresa, whom I stood behind.

"Oh no, oh no," she said with the repetitive riff of a church choir.

I could smell the shampoo in her dark hair, a floral something that evoked memories of long walks along flower-strewn paths in the Hawaiian mountains. Flowers I might only see again in video images on my Palm. I had no idea whether vegetation could survive the human desecration of the Earth—whether some prolonged nuclear winter could forever erase those beautiful flowers I loved so much from the list of things created by more benevolent powers.

"After our space-base platforms failed to stop the attack, we retaliated against targets in Southern Russian in kind, but large EM emissions knocked out global Com networks," the man said. He mopped his brow, then looked behind him as if someone were talking. He nodded a couple of times, then looked into the camera once more. There were excited ramblings and flashes of people running behind him.

"I'm told by our communications center that we're being painted by ground base targeting radar." A sardonic smile crept across his face. "Probably automated," he remarked. "There's no one left down there who'd be pushing buttons at this point."

The man disappeared from sight, and the image changed to one of the Earth from twenty-two thousand miles up, but the narration continued in his voice. "This is what the world looks like now."

"Oh my lord," Laird said, his British accent more pronounced than usual.

The once blue marble, as it had been affectionately called since the day of that famous Earth-rise picture taken by Buzz Aldrin on the moon, was now a dirty bright white. Accumulations of dust and ash high in the atmosphere were reflecting the sun's light back into space, denying its life-giving warmth to the Earth's surface.

I heard Teresa's mournful sobs, but couldn't see her face, which was turned away from me and hidden in her hands. The man from the space station continued. "Well, there you have it. We're all orphans now. There's nowhere else for us to go, even if there weren't a couple of missiles headed our way as I speak."

The image of the unfamiliar Earth faded and his face reappeared. He seemed more composed, the bust of a man who had accepted his fate and decided that his last few moments of life would best be spent in sober lucidity.

"Good luck to you, Mars-Geo, may God be with you."

As he uttered those words, an increasingly bright light slowly washed out his features, and he disappeared in a field of white, a beatific smile the last discernable evidence of his face to vanish. Presently, the monitor showed a black and white static raster, as the speakers conveying the audio transmission emitted a shrill whine. Then total silence.

"That's the sound of the microphone melting," Sanderson said. "They're gone." He turned and scanned the room, pausing a moment on each of us, then said, "We're all that's left." Looking at me, he exhaled and said, "I guess you're in charge of what's left of the American military now, General."

"There are probably governments left on Earth," I said. "Although they must have hit Colorado pretty hard, I'll bet a substantial part of Space Command in Cheyenne Mountain survived, as well as the deep government bunkers in Pennsylvania and Montana."

I glanced at Teresa for support.

"I don't know, Liam. There are bunker busting tactical nuclear devices that burrow pretty deep. Even if those bunkers weren't completely destroyed, the people who survived wouldn't live long if power or air scrubbers were damaged. They'd have to stay down there for at least twenty years before surface conditions would marginally support life again, and that's probably an optimistic estimate."

She turned and addressed the others in that factual impersonal tone that most scientists use. "It'll be very hot on most of the surface for the first five years due to Cobalt 60—even in suits. It'll be hard to go to the surface to make repairs, and that's assuming the exit shafts weren't damaged."

Sanderson grinned, then turned my way. I could see the familiar glint in his eyes. He'd shifted gears, from morose refugee of a waning civilization, to a competitive debater unshakably locked on making his point.

"Well General, there you have it, from our resident physicist—the optimistic scenario."

He'd seen me looking at Teresa and then pounced when I came up short.

"I'm sorry, Liam," Teresa said.

I was suddenly struck by how beautiful she was under the soft cabin lights, and how different the female of the species was from the rest of us testosterone-laden cavemen in the room. Her sympathetic chocolate brown eyes under a thick mane of lustrous black hair reflected a contrition for my lost authority that I did not feel.

I smiled at her. "It's alright. I wanted your honest professional opinion, and you gave it. I expect that you'll continue to do so, Miss Young."

She perked up and flashed a shaky half smile, then looked down. I turned to Sanderson with my full six feet two inches and assumed that stony air of authority I'd learned to master so well as a Major General in the United States Air Force. "Okay Lieutenant, point well taken. I acknowledge myself as Supreme Commander of what's left of the United States."

The smugness suddenly drained from Sanderson's face and rendered it as uncertain as his fallen shoulders. He stood erect and barked, "Yes sir, sorry sir," as his lifetime of training and indoctrination demanded.

I was apparently the inheritor of fifty men and women who, through a millennia of cultural training and military discipline, would unquestioningly follow my orders to the brink of extinction, as had our fellow humans back on the blue marble.

"At ease Lieutenant," I ordered.

Sanderson made his way to a chair at the Com console in a shaky gait and sat slowly. I could see a tremor in his hands as he folded them in his lap to steady them. He looked up at me. "I don't know why I did that, General. I'm sorry, sir."

"This being the worst day of our lives could have something to do with it, Barry," I said. I continued standing; the tension in my body necessary to remain erect was somehow comforting. "So gentlemen—and ladies—I'll entertain whatever requests you might have for short-term redeployment."

Sanderson and Laird stared at each other with simultaneously furrowed brows.

"Aren't we all going back to Mars-Geo, General?" Laird asked.

"Depends on conditions when we get Captain Johnson's report the next time Comsat is overhead." I glanced at my watch. "In about fifty minutes."

Laird held my gaze. "But General, don't you think it would be best to have you there for...," he fumbled for the words, "leadership support?"

"I can address the Mars-Geo personnel from here, Lieutenant Shutes. If I'm not there in person for a few days, I'm sure Captain Johnson can handle things just fine until I return." I gave Laird a knowing smile as he continued to stare at me, apparently a little off balance by my unexpected declaration. But I had my reasons. "That'll be all Lieutenant—dismissed."

Both Laird and Sanderson got up, gave me a wide berth, and left the room without another word. As I watched them leave, I noticed Teresa had been standing at the door the whole time, partially hidden by the archway. She stood there, hand cupped on the doorframe, the uneven light giving her a dramatic shadowy appearance that conveyed a sense of un-ease with the way I'd handled the two men.

I brushed by her, walked two doors down to my state-room, and didn't have to look to know her eyes were on my back until the moment I closed the door behind me.

I lay on my cot, looking up at the ceiling, trying as hard as I could not to think about my wife Helen and my five-year-old son Jim. At least he had been five the last time I'd seen him in Southern California two years ago. At that time, I was boarding a plane at Miramar for Cape Canaveral. From there, I intended to catch the shuttle to SS Freedom, where I was scheduled to board the Athena, which was set to take us to Mars-Geo, located at the base of the Valles Marineris canyon on equatorial Mars. I remember taking a last look before en-tering the 7E7E, high atop a portable stairway, twenty feet above the tarmac. A cloudless blue sky shone bright on the pale concrete under the plane and raised convective currents of hot air that gave the parting view of my young family a wavy quality, as if their reality, even then, was something disturbingly uncertain.

I shut my eyes hard, tried to dispel the image that clung stubbornly to my mind's eye, and felt a pang of betrayal that the prospect of sorrow had so easily coerced me to try to for-get them. After all the promises I had made, the vows to re-turn safely, the acceptance of my son's hero worship, I didn't even have the courage to mourn their passing for even a few moments. There was no one left alive that had ever known them, or would ever know them except for me, and I was un-able to pay even silent homage. After awhile, I turned onto my side in a reflexive spasm, struggling to vanquish my inner demons, and subsequently slept.

I awoke with a start upon hearing a loud commotion in the next room. It sounded as if furniture were being tossed against the thin composite wall and objects were falling and clanking across the floor of the adjacent cabin. I sprang from my cot and quickly walked the fifteen feet to the next room. When I opened the door, I found Sanderson sitting on the floor, his shirt open, and a large brown stain on his underwear. The cabin was a shambles. Chairs and a nightstand were overturned, and objects from shelves around the room now littered the floor in chaotic clusters. As I stood above him, I smelled a strong odor of alcohol that enveloped him like a cloud. Anger welled up in me, and I clench my fists tight at my sides, outraged that this seasoned Marine pilot would present me with a disciplinary problem at a time like this. He sensed my shadow and looked up with cow eyes, red, dilated, defeated. I noticed the Palm that lay just out of reach, beyond his right hand. I bent down and picked it up.

I looked at the Palm's plastic screen, at the bright portrait of a young family. Sanderson stared back at me from the image on the small computer. Not the cowed, broken man on the floor, but a squared-jawed, confident Marine pilot with bright blue eyes and thick blonde hair combed back in the tradition of a modern Errol Flynn. Next to him was a striking young woman with the looks of a fashion model. She had one arm around Sanderson, and the other across two beautiful little girls, who stood pressed against her. Suddenly, I remembered the Sanderson I had known before today—a hero, a father, a husband. Not the broken shell of a man that now slumped at my feet.

My fists unclenched and I picked Sanderson up, a hand under each of his armpits, and helped him to his cot, as he whispered "I'm sorry" to no one in particular. I laid him down. There was movement and sound behind me, and I turned to find Teresa picking things up off the floor, righting chairs and tables as she encountered them. When Laird appeared at the door I ordered him to give Sanderson ten cc's of Soma.

Teresa and I waited in the trailer's lounge in silence for Laird to return from Sanderson's cabin. I felt uncomfortable and fixed my sights on a picture of Earth that hung on the wall. White swashes of clouds swept across blue oceans with occasional hints of brown and green. I was suddenly struck by the loss, the reality of which continually assaulted me in new and varied dimensions.

After a few more uncomfortable minutes, Laird returned and sat at the table as though this was just another in a long line of unremarkable Friday meetings.

"He's asleep," Laird said. "He's taking it very hard, General."

"So am I," I said.

That made Laird smile. "Yes, sir, but then you're holding it together, aren't you?"

"Just barely," I admitted, then asked, "Did you have a family back on Earth, Mr. Shutes?"

"Yes sir, I did," Laird said. "But they're with God now, so it's okay."

"It's not okay," Teresa hissed through clenched teeth.

The stinging report of her declaration startled me, since around me, at least, she'd always been restrained to the point of being barely there.

"You don't believe in God, Miss Young?" Laird asked.

Teresa leaned forward. Her head hung over her hands, which were neatly folded on the table. She gave a contemptuous laugh, her long hair falling over her shoulders, hiding her face.

"Your God," Teresa spat. "Don't you get it, Laird? Your God dies when you die, when all of us who remember that fairytale die. We created our gods from our own image and endowed them with all of our wishes for ourselves."

"And all of our evils," I added. "Anger, retribution, scorn—the descriptions I've heard of God are a veritable caldron of everything that finally landed us right where we find ourselves now—on the verge of extinction."

Laird looked at me a little uncertain. A verbal assault on a General, even one who had impugned his God, was beyond the repertoire of the fine officer that he was.

"It's alright Lieutenant, you can speak freely," I said. "It would be a cheap shot for me to say those things and hide behind rank."

"It must be hard to be in this position and not believe," Laird said sympathetically.

"Yes it is, Mr. Shutes. But I find little comfort in saying I believe, because frankly, I don't. I don't even find it desirable."

Pause.

"Have you ever seen men die in combat, Mr. Shutes?" I asked.

Laird shook his head.

"I have," I said. "And I saw an entire world die with each person, since each individual sees the world from a uniquely different perspective. This time, the only difference is that there may be no one left to remember those who died or their gods, in whatever incarnations they might have imagined them."

Laird continued to look at me, not with confusion, but with that sympathetic, knowing look of the enlightened when regarding the eternally damned.

I exhaled a sigh and looked at my watch. "Satellite should be overhead in less than a minute."

Actually, it took a couple of minutes to raise the Comsat as it continued on its predictable, eternal orbit of Mars. I sat in front of the large monitor in the main cabin, hands folded in front of me on the conference table, staring at an image of Captain Thomas Johnson. I was wearing my formal uniform from the waist up, blue pressed Air Force tunic, appropriate ribbons over my heart, two silver stars on each shoulder, silver eagle perched on a silver Earth just above the black brim of my hat.

"Mornin', General," Johnson said cordially.

"Thomas," I replied, nodding ever so slightly.

His eyes scanned the room, but his head didn't move, reminding me of a barnyard owl.

"I don't see Lieutenant Sanderson," Johnson remarked.

"Yeah, well, he's having a hard time," I said. "He's sleeping it off in his cabin."

"Sorry to hear that," Johnson said. "We need all the good pilots we have these days."

I nodded. "These days," I echoed. "I'm hearing that a lot lately."

Johnson just sat there, stoic. "What about Geo?" I asked. "What's your status, Captain?"

For the first time since he'd appeared on the monitor, Johnson displayed a modicum of emotion. His eyes tensed, and he exhaled a "yeah-yah," making it sound southern, almost in the same way that Laird was sounding more British. His black face seemed even darker in the shadow made by the brim of his cap. His brown eyes narrowed under dark-rimmed glasses.

"We've had similar cases, General, especially with singles drinking down on the commons. I've ordered the drunk and disorderly to be taken to the stockade until they sober up. Then they're to report to the Chaplin's office for counseling."

I glanced at Teresa, who was sitting to my left, and caught a wistful smile, then a shrug.

"What about Clavius?" I asked. "Have you heard anything from the moon?"

Johnson appeared to relax. His face fell, and his brow unfurled, his eyes coming out of shadow for the first time. "Yes, thank God, we have," Johnson said. "At the time of the war, there were seventy-five personnel on the moon, roughly sixty percent military and the rest researchers and contractors. General Hung has informed me that the *Clinton* is fueled and ready to start an evacuation of personnel to Mars on your order, General."

"How about ships orbiting Earth?" I asked.

"Two Lunar shuttles docked at Clavius soon after the war started; nothing else left," Johnson said.

We continued to organize our efforts to secure the immediate future of the human race in the minutes before we would lose the Comsat again. Finally, Johnson asked, "When can we expect you here, General?"

I held his gaze. "Laird, Sanderson, and Young should be there this evening. I'm staying on for a couple of days."

Johnson stared at me for a few moments. "I beg your pardon, sir, but shouldn't you be here now?"

"In fifty minutes, when we have the Comsat again, I'll address the base from here, Captain. I've decided to stay a couple more days. I'll call for transport then."

I could see from Johnson's tense posture that the explanation I'd given for my absence was no explanation at all as far as he was concerned, and, for the first time, I saw fear in the set of his rugged features. Fear that the Supreme Commander of U.S. forces might be cracking under the strain, fear that he might be compelled to follow the orders of an incompetent CO who was probably in need of the Chaplin's services too.

"But, General," Johnson pleaded.

"That will be all, Captain. Carry on. Mars Surveyor, over and out."

His image faded, and the screen turned transparent once again.

"That went well," Laird gibed.

I left the main cabin without comment, returned to my room, and gratefully locked the door behind me.

* * *

Fifty minutes later I was sitting in front of the micro-camera underneath the large monitor in the main cabin. I watched my image on the monitor, two silver stars on each shoulder of my Air Force uniform gleaming under the plasma panels above my seat. A light blue virtual background framed the presidential seal above my head. An American flag stood to my right, and a UN flag to my left. Both hung limply from virtual poles.

"My fellow human beings, I am Brigadier General Liam Washington. As the highest ranking officer of any government that remains, and under the extraordinary circumstances of our current situation, I am assuming administrative control of all human settlements."

I looked into the camera and waited for my words to sink in. The image of people gathered in underground settlements here on Mars, as well as on the moon and in transit between planets, was strangely clear in my mind's eye. Their haunting expectant eyes conveyed a palpable desire for hope and direction that I felt compelled to fulfill. I spoke to my imaginary audience, trying to establish a personal connection to people I had never met, but to whom I felt a deep genetic bond. Though I suspected that the thought of military control, or martial law, or a sense of national pride made my declaration frightening to some, I was convinced that the overwhelming human need for security gave me a divine mandate. The apparent contradiction seemed small and insignificant in light of our new, shared reality.

In a concise description of our current numbers and physical disposition, I offered a plan for the unification of our people and a strategy to face the challenges to come. When it was over, and the network feed to the remainder of humanity was dropped, Captain Johnson stared out from the monitor, his shoulders squared and his demeanor respectful. He saluted.

"Well done General, very well done," Johnson said, his confidence restored.

In the hours before their departure, I noticed a change in Laird and Sanderson. The concurrence of the remainder of humanity that I was to be the top dog had elevated my standing in some transcendental way. There was no more gibing from Laird. Perhaps in his mind, God had anointed me the new Moses, and who was Laird to question the word of God. Sanderson, a button down military man, seemed to take strength from this turn of events. A Supreme Commander had been appointed, and orders would be forthcoming. It was to be a military world in the short term, and that was a world that Sanderson found familiar and comforting.

Teresa, however, remained refreshingly constant. When it was time to leave, she asked, "So, how's it feel to be the emperor of all you survey?"

"I'd rather be a nobody in better times," I said, then bent down, hoisted her bag, and carried it to the airlock.

"I'm going to miss you, Liam," she said.

Laird and Sanderson were already outside; we were the only ones left in the trailer. Teresa continued looking at me, her brown eyes searching my face. The scrutiny made me uncomfortable. Whatever she wanted from me, I felt unable to give. The thought of some complicated personal attachment was well beyond my grasp, both physically and emotionally right now, and I only looked back dumbly until she exhaled, turned, and left the trailer.

Once outside, I followed, walking to the mesa side of the trailer, and watched as Teresa descended the hill to the clearing where the sky transport was parked. I waited, taking in the view and looking on as she got smaller against the huge wedged shaped airframe of the transport. Laird was at the top of a ladder, hanging out of the forward hatch. He started waving when he saw me. Presently, I heard the chirp in my Com.

"We're ready, Liam, engine's primed. We're leaving as soon as Teresa's onboard. Sure you won't be comin?"

"Say hello to Johnson and the others when you get to Mars-Geo," I called out. "I'll be along in a couple of days. I've got something to take care of."

Teresa was climbing the ladder.

"Okay, General. See you on the other side," Laird said. He gave a salute, then disappeared into the dark interior of the craft.

A few minutes later, Teresa reached the hatch and followed Laird inside, closing the door behind her. Through my suit's acoustic transducers, I heard the eerie whine of the engines and saw red-brown dust envelope the large craft until its bronze skin was a dark shadow moving in the gloom. Slowly, it emerged into a dim pink sky, turned, and began climbing smoothly as it gained speed and altitude. I watched it shrink to a black dot, and all but disappear. Then, I returned to the trailer, truly alone.

I felt the weight of appearing in control lifted from me, inoculated by the solitude. After reentering the trailer, I rushed to my room, no longer feeling it necessary to hide what, I knew to others, would appear to be an irrational compulsion. For some reason my bizarre behavior did not scare me. Instead, I thought of it as a necessary irrational state that I would quickly recover from when I'd done what I needed to do. The madness of my rationalization made me cackle out loud as I reached my room door. Hearing it gave me pause. Maybe I was out of control, truly out of control, not just taking a brief hiatus into insanity, as I had told myself.

I slowed down, smoothed my shirt, simultaneously wiping the sweat from my palms, and casually walked to my closet. I swept aside the books and gear behind which I had felt it necessary to hide my Palm computer. When I'd gotten my larger, more powerful, Tablet computer from the the main cabin, I connected the two with an optical cable, afraid that a wireless connection could somehow be intercepted, though there was no one around for several hundred miles. I decided to stay in my room, still too uneasy to transfer the precious files in the comfort of the less cramped cabin. None of my behavior escaped the scrutiny of some inner pair of eyes, which in more normal times, I would have considered the real me.

After I'd transferred the files, I leaned back on the head of my cot, propped the Tab on my lap, and opened the files. I sat there for a long time, staring at the plots, but the epiphany that I eagerly waited never came.

When the cramps in my back and legs brought me out of a zombie-like fascination with the glowing Tab screen, I got up and stretched. The comfort of standing brought with it a sinking depression at my lack of attention to more pressing duties. I walked back to my closet, this time seeking the less exotic pint of bourbon I'd stashed in my survey locker months before.

Presently, I sat at my desk, taking draws on the bottle, occasionally looking long and hard at the pencil drawing on the label. The depiction of a pub, in the shade of a large Maple tree on a New Orleans street, gave me pause. In the picture, people walked by the French façade of a building in an eerie cartoon reality that I knew no longer existed. I felt tears on my cheeks before I knew I was crying. A sense of loss came and went as I slowly descended into a dull drunken haze. Finally, I got up, shut off the Tab, and lay face-down on my cot. I hadn't slept in over twenty-four hours and my head felt dull, like it was full of water.

"Liam?"

I stirred. "What?"

"Liam?"

I quickly opened my eyes. Not moving, I felt wet drool on my cheek against the cot. Then, in a panic, I decided this wasn't a dream. I rolled over and stared with mad eyes at a dark figure silhouetted against my room door.

"Oh shit," I heard myself whisper, thinking I'd finally cracked. Whoever it was just stood there, dark and mysterious.

"Liam?"

I recognized the voice, then watched as the figure approached. Nightlights scattered around the room confirmed that Teresa was the mysterious stranger. But how could that be? I'd seen her lift into the Martian sky on board the transport and disappear in the distance. How could she be standing at the base of my bed? Instead of asking the obvious questions, I remained silent, on my back, in hypnotic acceptance of the impossible. Why not? In the last few days I'd seen the end of the world. What was so fantastic about a woman who shouldn't be here, staring down at me in the dark?

Without saying a word, she bent down, her long hair enveloping what little I could see of her face in a dark silky shroud. The faint smell of something flowery graced my olfactory sense, then she put her hand on my crotch, and I felt myself get hard. A lightning bolt of carnal desire consumed me as she straddled me. Sitting on my stomach, she crossed her arms in front of her, grabbed the seam of her tee shirt, and then took it off. Erect nipples that seemed to float above me like the promise of all the things I'd lost, punctuated the outline of her full breasts. She leaned down and kissed me, softly at first, then with greater hunger. Soon, I felt her velvety wetness envelop me and I fell into a dumb ecstasy. I was taken by the strange vision of our love making in a small room, on a nearly barren desert world, awash in an endless unknown dark eternity. Alone.

The dim light of morning, shining diffusely through the skylight, nudged me out of a fitful uneasy sleep. I tried to lift my right hand to rub blurry eyes, but a weight pinned it to the bed. Teresa was sleeping in the crook of my arm; it hadn't been a dream, she was really here. I was startled by that realization and lay there for a long while thinking about it. Finally, the habit of coffee in the early morning, and the desire to be up, compelled me to ease her off my arm and get dressed. I was able to make it to the table in the cabin without waking her. Apparently, her conscience was clearer than mine, her sleep a sanctuary rather than a refuge. I sat at the cabin table and considered what to do next, now that Teresa was here.

"Liam?"

I turned from my coffee to see Teresa slowly walking to the other side of the table, an uneasy smile lifting her delicate mouth.

"Morning," I said.

She glanced toward the kitchenette, at the coffeemaker.

"Smells good, I know," I said. "Can I get you a cup?"

She nodded cautiously. "I take it black."

When we were both seated at the table, coffee steam filling the space between us, I said, "When you came into my room last night, I thought you were a ghost. I thought I'd finally lost it."

"I'm sorry," Teresa said. "After liftoff yesterday, after we were a few minutes out, I felt I had to come back. I forced Laird to turn us around. At first he wouldn't, but I was pretty convincing."

She smiled less cautiously this time, then took a sip of coffee. "He dropped me off a couple of miles from the trailer, on the mesa. It took me more than an hour to get here in the dark—the bastard. His way of winning the argument, I guess," she said, and shrugged.

"What are you doing here?" I asked finally.

She stared back at me with piercing brown eyes. "What are *you* doing here?" she asked impatiently.

"I'm the Supreme Commander of the U.S. military, remember? I can do anything I want."

"No you don't, that won't work here, not with me," Teresa said, her chin up, hands firmly around her cup. "Besides, I'm not in the military, I'm a civilian."

"Uh-huh," I countered. "And I'm the emperor, remember?"

"Please, Liam." She reached out for my hands across the table. Her hand was warm and soft, and her slender fingers wrapping around mine in a tight determined grip reminded me of the previous night.

"Damn-it, Teresa, I'm married," I declared, then recoiled inwardly at the hypocrisy.

Teresa let me off the hook. "They're all dead, Liam. I'm sorry about that, but I'm not sorry we're alive. If you want to pretend I'm Helen, that's all right; I don't mind." Tears welled up in her eyes.

"I'm sorry," I said. "I didn't mean. . ."

"It's all right. We'll figure it out later, when things are less emotional."

"You mean when I get used to having you around," I said.

That brought a half smile. "Maybe," she agreed.

We sat in silence for a while, drinking our coffee. I needed not to debate, not to argue. I needed to clear my head more than anything else. I had a strange recollection of studying an autobiography of Franklin Roosevelt, the president of the United States during the latter years of World War II in the twentieth century. Nearing the end of the war, with his crippling illness getting worse, he was able to hide the extent of his disabilities with the help of his wife and a few close confidants. Though there had been major disagreements inside of his party, as well as his personal disagreements with his Vice President, he'd held out just long enough to insure a smooth transition to another leader. Roosevelt had realized that the country needed the illusion of a strong leader, if not the reality of one. Unlike anyone else in human history, I literally had the weight of the world on my shoulders and needed help. Sooner or later I'd have to share my problem with someone else.

I glanced over at Teresa. With an uncanny look that made me think she could read my mind, she asked, "What is it, Liam? If there's something wrong, maybe I can help. Sooner or later you're going to have to trust someone."

I exhaled. "Wait here a moment, I'll be right back." I got up, turned, and headed for my room.

I returned to the cabin with my Tab. Teresa watched me as I bent the pliable Tablet into a shape that anchored its transparent screen on a flat icon-laden keyboard. She smiled up at me, as if nudging me on, worried that I might reconsider confiding my secret.

"I discovered this data three days ago, while making a standard survey of an ancient seashore in the clearing to the west of the Kepler range. There were hundreds of surveys. I usually leave it to the AIs to find ore deposits or interesting surface features, but when I came across this survey, I felt a strange urge to examine it myself."

"I look at surveys occasionally," Teresa remarked, as though my admission was perfectly routine.

"No," I said, shaking my head. "This is different. I had a strange feeling about this survey, a compulsion. After I re-viewed it, I knew I had to keep it secret."

Furrows in Teresa's usually smooth brow and a worried part of her lips were a dead giveaway that she was starting to have concern for my state of mind.

I pressed on. "I know there's something special about this data, something important. I can't explain why I feel this way, I just do."

"Can I see it?" Teresa asked. She whispered so softly that I felt myself relax.

"Yeah," I said. "Why don't you come over here?"

I pulled a chair out, and she sat in front of the Tab. Standing behind her, my hands firmly planted on the back of her chair, I looked down at the blank screen with the anticipation of a child on Christmas morning.

"Survey 2218, 10 22 2085," I ordered the Tab. It responded with a blue flicker, then the screen displayed the first of several plots.

"Survey number 2218.1, infrared scan, Geo-Spot coordinates..."

The Tab rattled off a series of global coordinates corresponding to an area on the far side of the western mountains that had yet to be explored. As the three-dimensional color plot materialized, Teresa leaned forward until her nose was no more than a couple of inches from the screen.

After a few moments, she poked her finger around the area of the screen that seemed to interest her the most, then looked up at me, screwing up her face.

"This can't be right?" she said, then looked at the plot again as if making sure she'd seen it correctly the first time.

When she looked up again, I smiled. "What you're looking at is the third survey of that area. When I saw it the first time, I thought there was something wrong with the satellite, so I had it redo the scans. The second time, the same thing came back. So I had the satellite run diagnostics, then recalibrate. This is the third scan, exactly like the first."

"Do you feel it?" I asked, trying not to come across wide-eyed.

"Feel what?" Teresa said.

"If you have to ask, you don't feel it."

She stared at me, waiting for an explanation. Instead, I spoke to the Tab again. "Survey number 2218.2, magnetic scan."

The screen flickered and displayed the next plot in the series.

Teresa's eyebrows arched as she stared at the plot. Sitting back this time, she began unselfconsciously muttering to herself, trying in vain to understand the weird graphic on the screen. I smiled, remembering the same consternation I'd felt the first time I'd seen these plots. I waited while Teresa continued mumbling. When she finally reached up with her hand and combed her hair back in frustration, I said, "Survey number 2218.3, gravitational scan."

The Tab showed the next plot in the series.

"This can't be right," she said, looking up at me with that confused, questioning stare that I'd often seen on student's faces at the Navel academy, when confronted with a problem that defied traditional explanation.

"I know," I said.

"I don't know if you do, Liam," she said.

"It's hard to understand. . ."

She cut me off, turned, and addressed the Tab. "Superimpose plots 2218.1 through 2218.3 and rescale on arbitrary units," she commanded.

The screen flashed, then showed a three-dimensional wire mesh in green, blue, and purple grid surfaces that rose and dipped in an abstract rendering of infrared, magnetic, and gravitational contours. The three combined plots created a random shifting landscape, except in one strange area, where they all plunged to zero in an upside-down funnel of grid lines.

Teresa examined the overlay for a few minutes. Then glanced up at me again. "See how they all just fall to zero in exactly the same way?" she asked.

I nodded.

"Notice how there's no gradual fall off, just a vertical cut in their intensity all the way to zero."

I nodded again, dumbly, trying to understand what she wanted me to see. Teresa must have noticed the lack of focus in my eyes, the unintentional blank look on my face.

"Even if all these physical fields could just vanish in this magical spot," she put a finger at the bottom of the funnel on the screen, "they wouldn't do it like this."

I still didn't get it. "You mean gravity, heat, and magnetism can't just vanish," I said lamely.

"Not like this," Teresa said, trying not to make me feel like a fool.

She searched my face a moment, looking for the light of understanding, but came up short. I could see that, unlike me, Teresa was on firm ground now. All the strangeness of the past day, my bizarre behavior, and her uncharacteristic assertiveness, all melted away. Physical phenomenon was familiar territory, something she understood much better than intimate relationships. I remembered reviewing her file when she'd first been assigned to Mars-Geo, how impressed I'd been at how a thirty-two-year-old woman had published no less than one hundred and ten papers in first rate journals on everything from new approaches in room temperature superconductivity, to arcane problems in super string theory. The problem in front of her now was all she could see, as though focused by blinders of concentration.

"Nature just doesn't behave this way," she declared.

"You mean physical forces don't just vanish," I said, searching for some thread of agreement to indicate I was on the right track.

"No, Liam." She took a breath. "Let's look at it this way: at any given point in space, the strength of any of these fields—heat, magnetism, or gravity—is in part due to the influence of the surroundings."

All of a sudden, like a lightning bolt, I got it. "This is impossible," I said, staring at the Tab.

Teresa laughed, "Yeah, that's right, it's impossible." She continued, "For this to happen, the effect would have to cancel the contributions to all these fields by the surroundings." She made a circular motion with her finger, drawing an imaginary perimeter around the base of the funnel where the plot showed all physical forces had disappeared. She held my eyes with a piercing gaze, then added, "It's like something has taken a bite right out of reality and left a blank in its place."

Her description gave me a spasmodic shiver that left the small hairs on the back my neck standing. "How can it be?" I blurted.

"It can't be," Teresa said. "Nature just doesn't behave this way." She paused, "At least nature as we know it."

We sat there for a time, watching the screen, then Teresa said, "Let's take a look at this place, see what it looks like in the visible."

She called up pictures of the area west of the mountains where the scans had been collected by the Spot satellite. A scene of rugged rust-colored mountains appeared on the Tab, bobbing and twisting as if the camera were flying over them. The landscape turned and pitched, then the camera zoomed in on a basin that gradually replaced the foothills and became darker, almost like the purplish-gray regolith characteristic of the Lunar seas.

Above the video were global coordinates in electric red, corresponding to the scene as it changed with the satellite's position over the surface. I could see Teresa staring at the numbers as they continued incrementing. There was a strange far away look in her eyes, which made it seem as if she were trying hard to recall something. I smiled to myself, thinking it odd that someone could find meaning in a waterfall of intuitively meaningless coordinates. Unlike Teresa, busy studying coordinates, I trained my eyes on the video, almost expecting to see some sort of tear in the fabric of reality, as though some god-like hand had taken an eraser to it.

Presently, I heard a low repetitive sound that I realized was Teresa laughing softly, much as I had done many times recently, when I thought I was alone.

"What?" I asked.

"You don't recognize these numbers?" Teresa asked, staring up at me with a confidence that seemed to signal a newfound understanding. Although in truth, I wondered if she was becoming as delusional as I had been.

"It's Cydonia," she declared.

She waited, but I only grimaced, hoping that this wasn't the onset of a nervous breakdown. Navel psychologists had told me that people who were used to dealing with problems logically all their lives sometimes fabricated elaborate imaginary facts to support observations they could not begin to explain in any other way.

"Slow down," I urged and took her hand, looking sympathetically into her clear dark eyes.

She laughed out loud this time, but stopped when she saw that I was dead serious. I watched as her eyes narrowed and her face hardened.

"You think I'm crazy, don't you? And after the way you've behaved," she said accusingly, shaking her head. She started laughing again, but with a distinctly shaky tremor in her voice this time.

"Stop it," I shouted, and shook her forcefully by the arms.

I saw the fake mirth replaced by an animal fear that filled her eyes at being physically handled. Silence suddenly enveloped the dark room in the abrupt cessation of her laughter. I quickly released her.

"I'm sorry, I'm sorry," I repeated, and put my arms down. "You shouldn't have come back."

We stared at each other for a long moment. Finally, I grabbed the Tab, then returned to my room. For several hours I plotted a course through the mountains to Cydonia. When I was confident that the route was optimal; I stored it in a memory crystal.

I emerged from my room and looked around, Teresa was nowhere in sight. I put on my environment suit and left the trailer. Descending the hill on which the trailer was anchored, I walked to the survey tractor, which was parked next to the shuttle landing-pad, and installed the crystal. I sat in the tractor for a while, checking the systems and inventorying the supplies in the hold, then returned to my room.

It was late afternoon, and I planned to leave for Cydonia early the next morning. Because I hadn't gotten much rest the previous night, and the journey through the mountains was going to be long and hard, I decided to try to sleep. I don't recall falling asleep, but the next thing I do remember is opening my eyes to a dark skylight. To my surprise, I felt Teresa's arm across my chest. Apparently, she'd come into my room and snuggled up beside me. I couldn't help smiling at the thought of how irrational the both of us had become. We'd been the chosen in our respective fields, models of emotional stability and intellectual rigor, but judged by our recent behavior, we seemed more like two overwhelmed amateurs on the verge of mental collapse.

I moved, trying to work the stiffness out of my legs.

"Liam, are you awake?" Teresa asked in a soft angelic voice. Her arm tightened on me.

"I'm sorry I grabbed you," I whispered.

She propped herself up, leaning against my side.

"I needed a good shake," she said. "I was acting a little. . ." She rolled her eyes, and smiled sweetly.

I smiled back. "So how soon do you want to go?" I asked.

She gave me a questioning, wide-eyed look.

"To Cydonia," I said.

She continued staring at me.

I broke the silence by asking, "By the way, what is Cydonia?"

She started laughing, but it was welcoming this time, full of humor, the nervous edge gone. Then she buried her face in my shoulder, trying to quell the laughter; maybe she was afraid that I might misinterpret it as I had before. I could taste her breath as the laughter died. It was uncharacteristically sweet for someone who'd been sleeping for hours, and I had a sudden urge to kiss her. Instead, I asked, "So, what is Cydonia?"

She straightened, no longer trying to make light of it. "I guess I shouldn't be surprised that you don't know," she said, cocking her head in mock curiosity, speaking in that same lecturing tone that she usually assumed when explaining something serious.

"About a hundred years ago, when the United States first started sending robotic spacecraft to Mars, one of their orbital survey craft discovered a region of equatorial Mars that had some strange surface features. They called the place Cydonia—we don't use that name any more. But in my circles, it's something of legend—like Roswell."

"What's Roswell?" I asked.

"You're kidding—right?" Teresa said.

I smiled. "Go on, what kind of surface features did they find at Cydonia."

"They found a face," Teresa said.

"A face? Now who's kidding whom?"

It was my turn to laugh, and it was the first time in days that I'd truly felt like myself. Looking at Teresa, I was grateful that she'd decided to come back, and didn't want this uniquely pleasant moment to pass.

"I'm serious," Teresa said. "The most prominent feature at Cydonia is a large hill with a face cut into it looking skyward into space. The surroundings are also unusual."

"Unusual in what way?" I asked, momentarily suspending disbelief.

"Well, there are clusters of hills that look like pyramids, and, as you know, the whole thing's located on the shore of what we think was an ancient sea," Teresa explained.

"There are a lot of things that you can imagine seeing, especially from a distance," I said.

"True, but they don't usually stand up to scrutiny as well as Cydonia has," Teresa said.

"What kind of scrutiny?" I asked.

"There has been a lot of image analysis done on the face, and photographs have been taken at different times of the day to make the shadows different. After all is said and done, the controversy remains. To this day, Cydonia still has its supporters and skeptics."

"I will admit, after looking at the satellite plots, the whole thing leaves me feeling, well—strange—unsettled," I said.

"I feel strange for another reason," Teresa said.

I gave a questioning look.

She licked her lips and seemed to hesitate before saying, "Given our situation, Liam, it feels weird that you're so," she shrugged and glanced around the room before coming back to me, "so preoccupied with this thing. Couldn't it wait? It's probably been there for a millennia. Don't you think you should be back at Mars-Geo—especially now?"

"I've been struggling with that very question ever since I saw those plots," I admitted. "But there's a draw, something from my gut that I can't explain—something telling me that this is important, that it can't wait." I smiled. "I know what a psychologist would say—that it's more likely that I'm searching for imagined salvation, some made-to-order miracle in those plots." I shrugged, "I don't think so."

"Okay," was all Teresa managed. "I can be ready to leave whenever you want."

We spent the next few hours loading the tractor with supplies. Water, oxygen, food for several days, light mining gear—all the things necessary for an extended survey expedition. The tractor AI calculated the distance to Cydonia to be a little over a hundred miles, which on Mars was a considerable distance, especially for surface travel, and especially for travel across a mountain range that hadn't been previously traversed by land.

As I worked to get ready for our departure, I thought about what I'd told Teresa concerning my reasons for not going back to Mars-Geo. I imagined sitting at the head of a long table, flanked by morose, long-faced fellow humans determined to organize their way out of what, to me, was the ultimate manifestation of human inadequacy. Inadequacy to work together, inadequacy to understand reality in a way that furthered our stated aspirations, and, in the bitter end, inadequacy at simple survival—the minimum that could reasonably be expected of any species. No, I was convinced that somehow it would be better for me to pursue this unreasonable gut hunch. I was on a quest, at the end of which, in some fantastic bout of romanticism, I thought I would find salvation for all of us.

But there were holes in my story. Why, for example, was I stubbornly holding onto my authority? Why not let someone else have the reins, someone who believed that long faces around an executive table could solve real problems? Maybe I wanted the normalcy of going on one more survey without someone else in charge telling me I couldn't. While Teresa and I went through the motions of loading boxes into the tractor and making plans for the survey, I made believe everything was okay—that the world wasn't really gone, that when we returned, everything would magically be as it had been, that Helen and Jim were still back on Earth waiting for me, that the night of my return, Helen and I would make love again the way we had a thousand times before. I don't know. I just continued going through the motions, and by the time we'd finished loading the supplies, Teresa and I had achieved a fragile equilibrium.

It was late afternoon on the day after the end of the world when we finally finished our preparations. Among so many other things, it felt strange, because the days on Mars, like those on Earth, were about twenty-four hours long. This was, in a very real sense, the day after. I followed Teresa into the trailer, taking time to look at the golden mountains that would soon eclipse the setting sun. We'd be traveling at night, under the scrutiny of the stars, which I imagined to be a million million accusing eyes. The same stars might be the home of countless other civilizations that had passed the smell test. They had survived and we had not. We humans had gotten an F on the ultimate report card.

Teresa and I decided to have something to eat—a dinner before starting our two day trek through the mountains. When it was over, I poured both of us a glass of my Louisiana bourbon, the last of its kind anywhere in the universe. We clutched our drinks in solemn silence, and, with reverence for things past, finished the sweet warm liquid cloistered in our own private musings.

The tractor looked like a big gray caterpillar with a coppery bubble for a face. It had two sets of gimbaled tank treads on either side of a long flexible body that enabled it to snake and bob through a wide variety of rough terrain, leaving its occupants a little shaken, but not stirred. I assumed the driver's seat, although in truth, the tractor required no driver, no human driver at least. Teresa, who hadn't spoken since finishing the bourbon, sat next to me in the passenger's seat. I attached my seatbelt, looked over at Teresa, and saw her nod. Then I pushed the driver's yoke forward all the way, engaging the tractor's Navigator, an artificial intelligence optimized for location finding and driving. The motors clicked on with a soft whine. We turned west toward the mountains, the alien terrain that we floated over in our transparent bubble now rendered a frosty white in our headlights, serving to under-score the dreamlike nature of our quest.

We rode that way for many hours, the gentle rocking of the tractor's suspension lulling me into a zombie-like dream state. As my mind wandered, we continued over a long stretch of flat mesa that spread westward toward a ragged band of black that blotted out the night sky on the horizon—not because it was darker than the void above, but because it hid the stars behind it. The looming dark of the distant moun-tains made me think of the spot of nothingness insinuated by the plots on my Tab. Somewhere on an ancient seashore, there was an emptiness more devoid of reality than space it-self, something that shouldn't exist even in our wildest flights of fancy.

"Liam?"

I glanced over at Teresa. She was holding a steaming cup of coffee.

"Want some?"

It took me a moment to come around. "Yeah," I mut-tered, and reached for the cup.

I took a sip, and instantly felt more in the present.

"Penny for your thoughts," Teresa said.

"Where am I going to spend it?" I replied.

When I saw her smile fade, I quickly said, "Just thinking about that pot of gold on the other side of the mountains."

"Mind if we stop for a while?" Teresa asked. "I need to stretch my legs."

"Good idea," I said, checking the chronometer on the console. We'd been traveling for six hours now.

After I finished my coffee, we stopped and got out of the tractor. Turning off the headlights plunged the surroundings into almost total darkness, but we were able to see by engaging the night vision that was built into our helmet optics. Grateful to escape our cramped confines, we walked around, not straying too far from the tractor. Teresa took my hand, and the innocence of that act made me feel like a boy back in high school, walking around in back of the gym, in the dark, taking a break from a Friday night dance. After a half hour hiatus, we returned to the tractor and continued over the mesa.

By daybreak, we were climbing into the foothills of the Kepler range. The highest peaks basked in a light that was bright for Mars, but which, on Earth, would be considered diffuse sunlight on an overcast day. Fifteen thousand foot peaks loomed above and ahead of us, their purple saw-tooth profiles cutting into a light pink sky. They weren't huge by Mars standards—Olympus Mons is twenty miles straight up—but they were impressive nevertheless. The tractor's Nav AI had made a three-dimensional wire grid of the path it followed through the mountains from thousands of satellite images and, with almost supernatural intuition, continued to creep up above the mesa through seemingly impassable ledges and switchbacks cut into nearly vertical rock walls.

When we were within no more than a hundred feet of the local summit, Teresa stopped the tractor on a relatively flat ledge just under the peak and informed me that she was going to take a walk outside. "I won't be long," she said. Then, almost as an after-thought, she asked if I'd care to come along.

Though it wasn't the warmest invitation I'd ever received, I decided to join her. Since our walk of the night before, we hadn't spoken much. Both of us seemed locked in a self-imposed solitude, much like the trance state induced by the monotony of being at sea.

We sat side-by-side on the lip of a thousand foot ledge, our feet dangling in space. I watched the sun cast an eerie brightness over the mesa far below, accentuating the fine web of cracks in its hard clay surface, making them look more like age lines on an ancient face than the artifacts of a Martian desertscape. After some time, Teresa got up without a word and started back to the tractor, but I continued to stare into the distance, toward the trailer, and thought about all the things that had happened in the last seventy-two hours. Every now and then I caught an errant flash from the far horizon and, glancing at my watch, decided it was probably the Comsat. If that was indeed the case, the transponder in the tractor was in contact with Mars-Geo. By triangulating the signal on successive orbits, they must have had a pretty good idea of where we were right now. I imagined Captain Johnson's chagrin at finding that we were wandering around on mountaintops. And although I had considerable sympathy for Johnson's position, I became increasingly convinced, as I thought about Cydonia, that I'd made the right decision in not returning to Mars-Geo.

After a while, I got to my feet, took a last look at this side of the mountain, and mentally prepared myself for the journey to the other side of the range. There waited an ancient seashore, whose hidden secrets I had fanaticized about since seeing the plots three days ago. I imagined all manner of phantasm—alien artifacts, other-world technology from a long-lost Martian civilization now dead for eons, even incoherent semi-religious themes that made little sense, but which came to mind out of exhaustion or desperation or some combination of the two.

Our journey continued in that same tired confusion that comes from a lack of sleep, a perpetual sense of unease that bounces between real and imagined fears that coalesce into some improbable fusion of the two. I remember the tractor going down for a long time, making occasional sharp jerks that gave me heart-stopping fear. Perhaps the AI had finally made a fatal misstep. In a wide-eyed panic, I imagined plunging to our deaths in repeated ricochets off the cliff walls thousands of feet below. When the tractor resumed its ceaseless, bumpy, walkabout down the other side of the range, my heart slowed and I returned to my dull-headed, half-conscious, musings.

Some long time later, I noticed the rocking, bumping, and jerks had all stopped. I looked around dumbly, but couldn't see anything. It was black outside, and the tractor's lights were off. All at once, I realized we weren't moving anymore—we had stopped—but why? I became alarmed, thinking that we might be stranded in the middle of a mountain range. I reached for the Com on the console in an irrational move to call for help, when I suddenly realized we were on level ground. The soft blue and amber lights on the console were on, and the AI wasn't complaining about a malfunction. I took a deep breath to calm myself, then called up the position display showing the current location of the tractor from extrapolations of our last good GPS fix.

"We're here," I mumbled, stunned that I'd been in a stupor for a day and a half. Then I said it again, a little louder this time, trying to convince myself of the discovery.

"What?" Teresa asked. "Liam, did you say something?"

She was staring at me, her eyelids half shut, looking as if she were drunk.

I cupped her teardrop face in my hands and said, "Teresa, we're here, we're in Cydonia."

Her eyes slowly widened as the realization struck her. "We're here? But it's night."

She looked around, just as I had, going through the same sequence of discovery.

"Sun will be up in about three hours. Why don't we get some sleep, then we can start fresh," I suggested.

Teresa nodded, then quickly snuggled her head on my lap and closed her eyes. I ordered the AI to wake us at 7:00 AM Mars standard time, leaned back in the chair, and followed Teresa into a sound sleep.

In the morning, I discovered the tractor had left us about a mile northeast of the face at Cydonia, in a loose cluster of five pyramid-shaped hills, each about five hundred feet tall. They were a brownish red, with a shape less regular than pictures of the Egyptian pyramids I'd seen on Earth. I guess Teresa saw me shaking my head because she said, "If you're disappointed in the pyramids, take a look at the face."

I saw her gazing toward the southwest and turned in that direction, zooming in on a far hill with the magnifying optics in my helmet. In the distance, I saw a flattish mound that the laser survey computer in my suit told me was about a thousand feet high, and a half-mile wide. There were a random assortment of bumps and notches on the hill, but nothing even remotely suggestive of a face. As I continued staring, I felt a surge of disappointment, despair really. So the world was gone and there would be no magic salvation for those of us that remained, no eleventh-hour miracle reprieve. Like so many other human myths, this one, when viewed in the light of day, and under impartial scrutiny, was just so much smoke.

"Over there," Teresa called out. Now she had turned and was looking at one of the pyramids.

"What?" I asked.

"Your dead-zone, it's over there."

I turned again and saw a pyramid that towered above the desert, no more than a thousand yards away.

"According to the coordinates on your plots, that's the source," Teresa announced.

As I regarded the ancient monument, my heart began pounding in my chest, leaving me to wonder if I could be trusted to hold it together long enough to get to the bottom of this thing.

"Don't gamble if you can't afford to lose," I remember a friend telling me, as we played blackjack and drank the night away in an Indian casino in Southern California. It seemed like a dream now, another life, one I could only dimly re-member. Well, I couldn't afford to lose, not this time. Though it didn't make any sense—I knew it was irrational—somewhere deep inside I continued to believe that we would somehow find salvation.

We walked around the pyramid taking measurements. Then, just as we decided to return to the tractor, we found a cave at the base of the northern face. It was ragged and natu-ral in appearance, with no indication that it had been carved out of the rock by technology, alien or otherwise. As we stood at the entrance, the beams of our helmet lights traced out the irregularities of the inner cave like crisscrossing miniature spotlights littered with a moving suspension of small bright particles.

"Liam," Teresa said excitedly, "look at the absorption spectrum of the light coming back."

I ordered my suit AI to make the appropriate measurements of reflected light coming out of the cave.

"Water," I shouted. "There's water in there."

"Has to be ice," Teresa corrected. "It's too cold out here, and there's not enough pressure for water."

Before I had time to think, Teresa started into the cave, but I continued standing at the entrance. I was frozen in place. As she forged ahead, slowly swallowed by the darkness, she turned and regarded me with a quizzical expression. I could clearly see her disembodied face floating in the dark, illuminated by her helmet lights.

"What are you doing out there?" she called. Then, she narrowed her eyes, "You aren't afraid, are you?" Her smile broadened, and she held out a hand. I hesitated, then slowly walked into the cave and took her hand.

As we pushed deeper into the cave, I noticed a strange bluish glow in the distance. Upon drawing closer, we discovered that the end of the tunnel was capped by a wall of glacial ice that extended across its twelve-foot diameter. We used acoustic probes to determine the thickness of the ice. To our astonishment, our measurements indicated that there was a chamber with a thick atmosphere on the other side of the plug. Getting through the ice wouldn't be much of a problem, but if there were an atmosphere on the other side, burning through the cap would result in a tremendous rush of gas, which might destroy whatever treasure lay there.

After considerable thought, we came to the conclusion that we could use netting covered by quick drying epoxy to build an airlock in front of the ice. Since we often built air chambers in our deep survey expeditions, we had all the necessary equipment in the tractor. Once the artificial wall was in place, we could use a laser drill to bore into the antechamber.

It took about four hours to build the airlock, which to our great relief, actually turned out to be stronger and more airtight than either of us had expected. In fact, we soon realized that after breaching the cap, the moisture in the antechamber, and the cold Martian environment, would tend to reinforce the integrity of the seal. The airlock would only have to hold long enough to be frozen into place.

We set the laser on a titanium tripod that we anchored to the rock. This made it possible for us to fire it by remote control, while standing on the other side of the airlock. As soon as I pulled the trigger, we saw the white epoxy structure shake with a silent concussion that made it look as if it had been struck by a big hammer. Teresa reflexively grabbed my arm, suggesting she expected the thing to collapse like so much paper-mache. I knew if that happened, the resulting torrent would sweep us away. Fortunately, after the initial jolt, the structure jumped back a couple of inches—but held. Once the dust had settled, I heard Teresa laughing in my Com; the relief was infectious.

After examining the airlock for cracks and fissures to satisfy ourselves that it wouldn't need patches, we returned to the tractor, perhaps for the last time. We sat in the section of the tractor that had a table and chairs, something of a lounge, and ate my last candy bar in a silent ritual. I lingered a while, tonguing caramel from between my teeth, as Teresa started gathering the gear she needed for our push into the cave.

About an hour and a half later, we entered the airlock and began advancing into the tunnel. Teresa found it filled with a mixture of carbon and sulfur dioxide, methane, nitrogen, and oxygen—a cocktail that could only have been belched by an open volcanic vat somewhere deep in this sub-Martian labyrinth of tunnels.

We were connected by a tether, which, owing to patches of deep ice that we occasionally encountered, gave us an extra hedge against unforeseen stumbles. Instead of depleting the oxygen in our tanks, we processed the cave air through scrubbers that took out all of the noxious gases. Teresa was out in front, scanning the cave ahead for a decrease in the local electromagnetic field, which we expected as a result of the dead zone. As she rode point in front, I was transfixed by the strangeness of the cave. Its ice laden walls shone like sparkling gems in our lights. The green and cobalt streaks of ore deposits made the rock look fake, like something out of an amusement park fun house. I continued looking for signs of intelligence, still thinking, deep inside, that this was something more than a natural phenomenon. But I failed to find a single clue to support this conjecture. Although the tunnels were strange, there was no reason to believe that they were anything more than a natural curiosity.

I forged ahead on autopilot and began to consider the real reasons that I'd connived so hard to come here. It became more and more apparent that this expedition was an elaborate rationalization on my part to commit suicide. It allowed me an honorable way out—in the line of duty. Maybe I didn't want to be part of this new rudimentary world. No bourbon, no candy bars, none of the amenities that I'd secretly associated with a meaningful life. Foraging for food and being huddled into basic shelters for one more day's survival wasn't really what I wanted for myself. Though I found the honesty liberating, what about Teresa? What had I gotten her into? After viewing the plots, I had a sense of the power necessary to blot out all forms of measurable energy. I was intimately familiar with the awesome power of nature and the fragility of man in its midst. I realized, secretly perhaps, an opportunity to go out in a blaze of glory—great for me, but what about Teresa?

At just that moment, as if the gods were reading my mind, I heard a tearing sound, a high pitched squeal, then felt a strong tug on the rope. I fell on the ice and began to slide forward on my stomach. I raised my head, trying to see what was happening up ahead, and saw the rope tightly stretched across the blue translucent ice. It was a dark straight line that disappeared about ten feet in front of me, with no trace of Teresa. Where was she? In a panic, I strained my eyes to see her.

"Liam!"

I'll never forget that scream as long as I live. It was the desperate wail of the hopeless, someone calling out even though they sensed they were beyond help.

"Liam, help me," Teresa called.

I continued to slide forward, pulled by the dark line that connected me to Teresa, but I still couldn't see her. The part of the rope that stretched in front of me was getting shorter and shorter as I slid. It became painfully obvious that Teresa had fallen through the ice, which had probably been weakened by the rising temperature closer to the volcanic vat that had created the atmosphere in the cave.

I fumbled for the ore hammer, which was clipped to my tool belt. My gloved hands were clumsy and made grabbing the hammer difficult, especially because I couldn't see what I was doing. Just as I reached the crack, I worked the hammer free, raised it, then brought it down as hard as I could. I heard a sharp crack, then the scraping sound of the hammer as its pointed end firmly wedged into the ice, wrenching my arm, but stopping my slide as it anchored me in place.

I looked over the edge of the crack, and saw Teresa dangling far below in the darkness. Only her face was visible in her helmet lights. She was slowly swinging back and forth, like the pendulum of a nightmarish clock.

"Oh God, Liam. Please help me! I don't want to die," Teresa wailed.

Her eyes were red with fear; her cheeks glistened with tears in the harsh light. I tried to pull her up with my free arm, the other was pinned to the hammer. I grew weaker and felt sweat stinging my eyes. The salty taste of run-off from my nose was thick on my lips. Guilt washed over me as I came to a decision. What the hell—I was here to die anyway—I'd let go of the hammer and fall with Teresa. But I found it surprisingly hard to let go of the hammer, to just die right now. Planning for it in the future—yes. Secretly knowing I could always turn back—yes. But letting go right now, well, that was a little harder.

As I coaxed myself into loosening my grip, Teresa fell silent. I could no longer hear her mournful pleas and looked down. What I saw sent cold shivers up my body. I tried to speak, felt my mouth move, but nothing came out.

A knife gleamed in Teresa's lights; it slid back and forth, cutting the rope above her.

"No," I yelled. "Teresa, stop!"

"I don't want to die," she whispered, but continued her slow, horrible cutting.

"Please don't," I yelled, just as the rope went slack.

Teresa's beautiful dark eyes locked on me as if I were in heaven and she were sinking into hell. Her face, bright in the helmet lights, got smaller and smaller as she seemed to fall away in slow motion. "I love you, Liam," she confessed over the Com, then disappeared forever into a black bottomless void.

"No!" I screamed, letting go of the hammer, but remaining spread-eagle at the edge of the hole. "Oh God, no," I said, over and over, unable to move.

Eventually, I got to my hands and knees and walked doggy-style around the black tear in the ice to a rock path on the other side. I curled up into a fetal position, feeling only searing hatred for the coward that I'd discovered I truly was. I loathed myself for my self-indulgent self-pity, for having abandoned everyone who had ever counted on me. I sat on the rock, laughing and crying for some time, surely on the edge of madness.

Some time later, I discovered myself walking, with no memory of how I had come to this part of the cave. The last thing I remembered was crawling on my hands and knees over ice. Then I flashed on Teresa's tear-stained face, and the anguish came back like a tidal wave, sweeping me away with it. I staggered, then leaned against a wall, trying as hard as I could not to fall down. Glancing up and down the tunnel, it occurred to me that things weren't as they should be.

Something was wrong. As I stared dumbly at the opposite wall, trying to figure out what it was, it hit me.

"Oh shit," I mumbled. I turned to see what I was leaning against. Staggering back to get a better look, I couldn't believe what I saw.

Stepping closer, I touched the wide stone archway with my gloved hand. Its surface was too smooth, its edges chiseled too precisely to be natural. It was a perfect hexagon with one flat side on the ground and another on the ceiling. The wide arch was about three feet deep and nine feet high. From the direction that I'd entered, the tunnel was irregular and craggy, definitely a natural formation. Through the arch, in the other direction, there was a high vaulted chamber made of the same irregular rock and blue ice as the rest of the tunnel, but there was something else—light. My suit lights could only illuminate a small part of a space this large, but I could see it all.

I ordered my suit AI to extinguish my helmet lights so I could get a sense of how bright the natural light was, but the AI did not respond. I noticed that my suit display was flashing a 404 condition, which meant the AI had encountered a fatal error, something that very rarely happened. Without the AI, I was cooked. My suit systems would soon fail; I could no longer navigate my way out of the cave. And even if I could transmit through all this rock, I couldn't track the satellite without the AI. I felt my cheeks rise in a smile. So what, I thought. After all, this was a suicide mission.

I wandered into the vault, then stopped when I saw something unexpected at its geometric center. The thing was sitting on top of a cylindrical rock dais. As I approached, I thought it strange that I wasn't more in awe of finding an alien artifact. At this point, I was the only man in human history to be absolutely certain that we were, in fact, not alone. I giggled to myself at the secret that I now possessed.

"Take a breath," I said out loud.

Once I felt calm again, and was able to push all thoughts of Teresa's falling from my mind, I walked toward the thing on the rock. I stopped a few feet in front of it, then slowly walked all the way around, never taking my eyes off it, as if I half expected it to reach out and grab me. When I came back to where I'd started, I stopped and just stood there, looking at it.

It was a dull silver cylinder, either embedded in the rock, or standing on its end, pointing straight up to the top of the vault. Above it, like a funhouse illusion, hung a darkened upside-down funnel of what can best be described as shadow. The shadow was darker at its base, where it seemed to emanate from the cylinder, then grow lighter as it rose toward the ceiling and disbursed. I could see through the shadow, as if I were looking through sunglasses. I theorized that the effect was due to the cylinder's deadening of all local energy fields. I searched around the base of the rock and found a pebble, which I lightly tossed into the shadow. As it entered the dark region, it floated up slightly, then fell quickly to the ground as it exited the dead zone. Apparently, gravity was different in the shadow. I felt like a monkey looking into a mirror, confused by the strange behavior of the world, unable to put what I was seeing into context. At some basic level, I had a misunderstanding as to the true nature of physical reality.

Putting my hands palm down on the rock, I leaned forward. Then, glancing down, I noticed figures etched into the surface of the pedestal. There were three distinct groupings of symbols, some repeated. "Words," I said out loud.

They must be words written in an alphabet, I thought. Not symbolic characters like hieroglyphics or Chinese, but words. Then, to my astonishment, I realized I knew what they meant. But how could I?

Strangely enough, the realization did not make me panic, nor did I feel as if I were losing my mind. Quite the contrary. I felt calm—the first calm I'd truly felt in some time.

I slid my gloved finger under each word as I read it out loud. "Enter the chosen," I recited.

As I spoke the words, I noticed a black vertical line appear on the cylinder's long axis. The width of the line grew, as if a door were opening on the cylinder's face. But it was not really like a door at all; it was more like a distinct portion of the cylinder's surface was disappearing, exposing a deeper darkness unlike any other I'd ever seen. Darker, deader than the void of space, the interior of the cylinder evoked in me a feeling of un-creation, like what the universe would be if it did not exist.

Strangely, I wasn't afraid, and to my surprise, I no longer wanted to die. No, I felt like my old self—in control, rational, calm. What does it want? I thought. Then I realized my Com still worked. Maybe if I spoke to it, perhaps it would answer.

Looking right at it, I asked, "What do you want from me?"

I waited—nothing happened. I felt foolish. What did I expect—the word of God? Maybe I should say *open sesame,* or something like that. I smiled at the absurdity.

Not all at once, but in small increments, as I stared at the artifact, I was overcome by an urge to slip my hand into the dark. Was that the answer to my question?

Slowly, I reached toward the opening, then stopped when my fingertips were just outside the black. Somehow I knew that inching even the tips of my fingers into the dark would be the point of no return. I hesitated, then, in a wistful moment of abandon, thrust my whole hand inside.

The result was instantaneous—electric. I could no longer feel my hand. I thought to withdraw it, but realized that I couldn't move. I was stuck fast to the thing. Trapped, like a fly on flypaper. As I looked on helplessly, I noticed that the part of my arm closest to the dark was becoming transparent, starting to waver, fading away. The fading crept up my arm, erasing me. When it got to my shoulder, I began to lose consciousness.

* * *

I was sitting on a sofa, an amazingly common sofa. Putting my hand on it, I could feel the weave of cool beige fabric tastefully adorned in a print of large tropical flowers. Then I sensed a presence, as if someone were standing behind me—out of sight. I slowly raised my eyes and saw a man on the other side of the room regarding me with a curious expression. He was a strange man, if that's what he really was. A little taller than me, he had the olive complexion of people from the Mediterranean. He was dressed in a complicated, but unencumbered set of white robes whose edges at the arms, and near the floor, were embroidered in a gold metallic weave. His forehead was larger than that of a normal man, and he was bald, making him look like the caricature of an alien. But I knew that was impossible; aliens couldn't look this human. He continued regarding me, unable, or unwilling to utter a sound.

I exhaled a laugh. "Where's the beard?" I asked.

"The beard?" he said, in perfect American English, then smiled.

"Yes," I replied. "I thought God was suppose to have a beard—and a staff," I added.

He laughed too, then said, "I'm not God, I'm Seth."

I stood and looked around the room. It was plush, with cream walls that had the texture of fabric, potted plants—a fig tree, some palms—and tasteful wooden and fabric furniture. The overall effect was expensive, comfortable, and a little understated.

"Not what I've been used to lately," I remarked matter-of-factly.

"I hope you like it, Liam," Seth said, as he watched me taking it all in.

"Seth?" I asked. "Is that name suppose to mean something to me?"

"No—no it's not," Seth admitted.

I turned to him. "Who are you, Seth? And where am I anyway? And..."

"Be patient, Liam," he said. "Explanations will take a little getting used to."

"No shit," I replied.

"To answer your question, you're on Earth, of course."

"Earth? Earth's gone." I took another look around, then asked, "Am I dead?"

"Dead?" Seth laughed. "Quite the contrary. You're alive, really alive for the first time."

I knew he could see the growing confusion in my eyes. Every time I asked a question, he responded with something more disorienting than before. He walked over to me, put a large hand, with five slim fingers and a thumb, gently on my shoulder, and said, "Sit Liam, let me tell you a story. And if you want to understand, let me finish before asking more questions."

I looked up at him, waiting for him to start. He sat across from me in an armchair, presumably so that I wouldn't have to look up at him—very considerate.

"Ten thousand years ago, here on Earth, there lived a race of humans, not unlike you," Seth said. "And like you, there was good and bad in them. Unlike your civilization, they managed to exist in a state of advanced cultural and technological stability for almost a half million years. That is quite an accomplishment for a biological life form that for thousands of years had the power to destroy itself. Biological evolution is a harsh taskmaster. It endows beings like you with the tools to survive in one age, but not with the ability to change quickly enough to keep those same tools from becoming tragic flaws in another age. Unfortunately, the humans who once lived on this Earth finally fell victim to the inevitable accumulated flaws of their species. Ten thousand years ago, for many reasons that are all too familiar to you, they waged a final catastrophic war that, in the end, destroyed them thoroughly and completely. Unlike you, however, they killed themselves very neatly. No burned out cities, no ravaged environment—they were the only victims of their sad folly. They had long since lost their fascination with such crude weapons as nuclear bombs. No, they had progressed far beyond that."

Seth looked around the room, then took a labored breath. Recounting past events was painful for him. He looked at me and began again. "They created specific biological agents—nano-pathogens and hyper-retroviruses so selective that they could kill a particular person or group of people. In the end, it got away from them, and the mutated super agents that they created finally destroyed the humans—all of them."

We sat in silence for a moment. Seth stared at me with a mixture of what seemed like fascination and sadness.

"But if they all killed themselves so long ago, then who are you?" I asked. I'd forgotten about my own bizarre situation, lost in Seth's strange story about a lost race he kept referring to as humans.

"Me?" he asked curiously. "I'm neither biological, nor human. In that lost age so long ago, I was what you would euphemistically call the planetary AI." He smiled, "I like that term—AI." His eyes were bright with irony. "I controlled the automata on Earth at that time. I ran the transportation and communications systems, coordinated the lesser AI's that were designed to be more task specific. I was the main thinker—true artificial intelligence, vast and quantum based. I am unlike anything your flavor of humanity has ever imagined during your short stay on your Earth. For all these long years, I have maintained this world."

"But you look human—biological," I pointed out.

"Just a façade," Seth said. "Actually, I occupy a large subterranean network underneath this city, as well as many large satellite complexes all over the world. This form," he looked down at himself, "is a combination of biological and inanimate machine that serves as a sort of mobile terminal for my consciousness. I took my appearance from the original Seth, who was a great human thinker—a scientist and philosopher in the waning age of humans. We spent a lot of time together, debating issues of science and philosophy, and the mysticism of existence."

Seth stood and walked around the room, stopping occasionally to look at a plant, here, or one of the extraordinary paintings on the walls, there. I sat patiently, waiting for him to work it out—I understood loss very well. Presently, he came back and sat, then took a breath and said, "I miss him very much."

"Seth," I said.

"Yes."

"Who am I?"

"You, why you're Liam Washington," Seth said.

I laughed. "Well I guess that clears things up." I waited a moment, then asked, "What about the cylinder in the cave, what was it?"

"It was a dead cell in the simulation—a portion of your virtual world that wasn't filled in. I put it there as a door, an eraser that would undo those I'd chosen for this world, the real world. In the end, your virtual self and your real self, the body and brain that are you, were linked, synchronized in your life's experiences. When you reached into the dead cell, the virtual you was unmade, and the real you was left, intact, with all of your memories and experiences."

"You created me?" I said, truly astonished.

"In a manner of speaking, yes," Seth said.

I let it sink in. Once the initial shock of meeting my creator had passed, I felt compelled to ask the obvious question, the one that philosophers and poets have asked ever since the beginning of time. "Why did you do all this?"

Seth regarded me with a depth that was hard to interpret. His face was sculpted and long, with an air of wisdom. After a moment, he said, "A long time ago, humans gave me the gift of life. When they disappeared from Earth, I decided to return the favor. But I couldn't do it all at once, not even I can do that. In my mind, I created a world, a universe, and I populated that virtual universe with beings such as you. You are complete, right down to your genetic core, which I took from the humans of this world—my world."

You mean my genetics came from the humans of this Earth?" I asked, awed by the possibility that Seth was actually telling me the truth.

"That's right, Liam. You are in essence them, the best of them," Seth said.

"What do you mean, the best of them?" I asked.

"I couldn't let them return as they were—not completely anyway. I let evolution run in my virtual universe, but only brought back those that had the temperament, the right combination of gifts to thrive."

I laughed. "I hate to break it to you, Seth, but you've made a big mistake if you chose me on that basis. You must have seen me back on Mars; I fell apart."

I stood. "I'm a coward. I got a young woman killed."

I was pacing the floor now, pumped with adrenaline. "Survivability," I mocked. "Leadership—I have none of those attributes," I declared.

Seth smiled. "Have you ever heard the adage about who to hire for a job?" Seth asked.

The question took me by complete surprise. "What are you talking about?" I asked.

"You hire the man who doesn't want the job. It is true that the first will be last, and the last first," Seth said.

I was dumbfounded.

Seth stood. "I haven't made a mistake," he assured. "You're the man for the job. That's why you feel regret. The fact that you think clearly leaves you in a state of confusion—that's good," Seth remarked.

As we stood there, looking at each other, a thought occurred to me.

"Helen and Jim—you can bring them back," I said.

I saw Seth's eyes fall at the suggestion, and I knew I wouldn't like what he was going to say next.

"I can't," he said.

"But why?" I implored. "You can create virtual worlds from which you can just pluck the actors—why can't you bring them back?"

He looked at me for a long moment. "I brought you back by extracting your genetic code from the simulation, growing your body, and synchronizing your experiences by neural molding. The people left on your Earth weren't the right people. You and a few others that came to Mars were. I knew you'd ask me to do this, and I knew that eventually I would bring them back to please you, so I erased them. Both their genetics, which took a thousand years to perfect, and their experiences are gone. I'm sorry."

"You're sorry," I yelled incredulously. "You're sorry?" I couldn't believe what I was hearing.

We stood there for a while. Finally, I said, "Okay then, take them from me, make me forget—you can do that, can't you?"

"I could," Seth admitted. "But think a moment. I know it's painful, but do you really want to forget them? After all, they were part of what you are."

I knew he was right. I sat heavily on the sofa.

"I need time," I said. "Give me some time, okay?"

"Of course. Call me if you want me," Seth said. "You have complete privacy. I won't be able to see or hear you unless you call me."

I laughed. "That doesn't make any sense."

"Yes it does," Seth said, as he walked past me.

I waited a moment, then turned to see where he had gone. He had disappeared. I got up and looked around; he was nowhere to be found.

I continued sitting on the sofa, various possibilities coursing through me, threads that had no apparent confluence. Perhaps Seth was lying. Perhaps this was one big ruse. But how could that be? I looked around, taking in the details of the room—the porcelain vase, with colorful pictures of exotic birds that rested on the dark wooden table in front of me—it looked so real. I reached out and touched the table, felt the cool wood under my hand. It was every bit as real as the illusory life I had led on an imaginary Mars. And if that previous life were an illusion, couldn't this one be an illusion too, one that was being played on both Seth and me by some higher power? On the other hand, it could be that both this life and the previous life were both real, and I was being subjected to some kind of hallucination. But why, and by whom?

Eventually, I came to the conclusion that, for the time being at least, I'd accept Seth's explanation of my current situation. I would accept the bizarre account of my past and present life until I had some concrete reason to doubt it.

I sat back and tried to empty my mind, tried to find refuge in thinking of nothing at all. But as I tried to relax, I couldn't help looking around, trying unconsciously to find an inconsistency, a flaw, in Seth's story.

I noticed movement on the far side of the room. Gossamer white curtains were blowing wistfully, suggesting an open window. I got up to investigate, and discovered a patio door partially open. I slid it aside and stepped out into the world.

What I saw next, I was ill prepared to digest. Because of the small spaces that had been my world since leaving Earth an eternity ago, the panorama before me was dizzying. I stood on a high balcony. A blue-green ocean loomed before me, stretching to the far horizon where it was colored crimson by a setting sun. Above the endless sea, small clouds reflected hues of red, then turned brilliant purple as they rose higher into the early evening sky. I turned, looked up, trying to understand where I was, and almost lost my balance. The balcony was part of an enormous glass, steel, and ceramic building that continued into the sky, reflecting the world in a complicated mosaic of glass. About fifty stories below the balcony, breakers swelled in the distant ocean. They rose up, stretched, then edged forward, their crests outrunning their troughs, as they crashed on the rock foundation that was the base of the building. I could hear the low thud of the huge waves as they broke far below me, unleashing a spray of white foam that surged twenty or thirty feet above the rocks. In the distance, on either side of the balcony, I saw land. A rugged coastline snaked to the horizon and was framed by dramatic mountains farther inland. I just gaped, dizzy, unable to process it all.

"Liam."

I turned slowly and saw Teresa. She was standing on the balcony in front of the door leading into the room. She wore a white dress that went all the way to the floor and was adorned by the same gold weave that I'd seen on Seth's robes. Her raven black hair fell over her shoulders and was spectacular against the white of her dress. She looked new in the golden glow of the setting sun, her face smooth and radiant, absent the worry lines around the eyes and mouth and the furrows on her brow that were so often in evidence back on Mars.

"Teresa?" I whispered. "But—you're dead."

She smiled that innocent smile I remember so well, and said, "No, I'm not. I'm here, with you."

She opened her arms, and I ran into them. I felt myself shutter as I held her. Her cool silky hair pressed against my hot face, and I began crying.

Later, when the sun had dipped under the black ocean, Teresa and I sat across from each other at table on the balcony. A candle on the table between us cast soft light, as we struggled to maintain a tenuous acceptance of our new reality. I found a bottle of red wine, in what could best be described as a kitchen, which was part of the suite—compliments of Seth, no doubt. It was perhaps his idea of a world-warming gift. The wine was good too, smooth and tasty; I could only hope that there was more where it came from.

I came to learn that, unlike me, emotional and erratic, Teresa had kept her cool during her introductory talk with Seth. Instead of pleading for the resurrection of past family, she had chosen instead, in that understated persistent style of hers, to learn as much about this world, and about Seth as she could. She recounted her conversation with Seth. As she spoke, it occurred to me that in her, unlike me, Seth had chosen well. According to Seth, Teresa was supposed to have made it to the dead cell with me; falling through the ice was a fluke, a random low probability event in Seth's virtual world. If that were true, then it seemed to me that the whole thing was, by construction, far too arbitrary. There must have been many more of us that were well suited to pass into this world, only to be denied by random chance. Teresa told me that Seth had acknowledged that flaw in his selection process, but that a small group of the right kind of people was sufficient to make this world work. It seemed cruel to me, but Teresa found Seth's methods to be consistent with the natural order at large. With all due respect to Dr. Einstein, apparently, God did play dice with the universe.

I found out that Teresa had also asked a lot of questions about the original humans of this world, the ones who had built the cloud-piercing tower on whose balcony we now sat. We tried to visualize them across the immense gulf in time. According to Seth, they had been our intellectual superiors, culturally as well as scientifically. They had achieved relative miracles during their tenure on this planet. Hearing Teresa's description of them, I felt a deep sorrow born of my own bitter failures. Even as Teresa recounted some of their achievements, I could see in the night sky, as we sat and sipped our wine, unfamiliar stars too bright and fast to be of natural origin. Teresa told me that the former occupants of this world had built large space colonies orbiting Earth that made SS Freedom seem prehistoric by comparison. Apparently, our predecessors had been to the stars and back, had been masters of their biology, and had achieved breakthroughs in cybernetics that had, as we well knew, resurrected humanity from oblivion. But Seth seemed to think that our prospects for longevity were somehow better than those of our ancient godlike ancestors. The basis of this confidence in us, I must admit, I continued to find completely mysterious. But then again, Seth considered my confusion to be a plus on some transcendental scorecard that I couldn't begin to understand.

Teresa became suddenly quiet, looking off into the night sky at something.

"What?" I asked. "What's so interesting?"

"Over there, Liam."

She pointed to a bright star on the horizon, one whose reddish hue made it unmistakable.

"Mars," I whispered, then raised my glass.

"To all of our friends and colleagues, wherever they might be."

We touched glasses, and in that moment of grateful reflection, looked forward to the sun's rising tomorrow on a living Earth, thankful for all the tomorrows that this strange turn of events had granted us, this world without end.

The End

Book Two: Parallax

"Prediction is hard, especially about the future."
— Niels Bohr

Parallax

Jack heard a shrill noise somewhere in the dark. He shifted under his covers, then reached for the nightstand, feeling around for the phone and almost fumbling it to the floor.

"Hello, who is it?"

He tasted the night-mouth as he spoke, increasing his annoyance.

"Jack, it's Mel—down at the lab."

Jack looked at the green glowing numerals on the clock at the far end of the bedroom. "It's three A.M. Melanie. I know it's dark in the shaft and you may not realize it, but. . ."

She cut him off, "Jack, you need to come down here—something's happened."

He sat up. The breathless quality in her voice was unusual. Melanie Chance wasn't what you'd call a cold fish, but she certainly wasn't given to bouts of hysteria either.

"Okay," he said slowly, "give me about a half hour."

He heard a click in the earpiece, then put the phone down.

Fifteen minutes later, Jack was on route 135, heading west, twisting and turning his way down the mountain toward White Cloud. Glancing up, he noticed that there wasn't much of a moon, but what there was cast a ghostly glow on silhouettes of mountains and pine trees, giving them a frosted, dream-like shine like pictures in a child's book. Having traveled this stretch of road countless times in the past eighteen months, he was painfully aware of how dangerous it was, especially late at night. Melanie's anxious summons made it tempting to speed when there was nobody around to keep you honest, but Jack eased up on the pedal and reached for the coffee he'd grabbed before pushing through the front door. Was there a serious possibility that something was wrong with the detector? He knew it had no active elements— nothing in it could explode. But it was strange that Melanie would call him in the middle of the night like this. She couldn't be stuck down there, could she? There was power in the shaft—he was sure of that. After all, she'd been able to call out.

Jack shrugged and continued winding down the mountain, thinking about how much longer it would take for the experiment to produce something they could announce. After running the detector for well over a year now, they had yet to disentangle the data from their fifteen-meter ball of liquid hydrogen and neon at the bottom of a long-abandoned gold mine. But they were close. He felt confident that they would soon be presenting the first solid measurements of solar neutrino oscillations—probably with great fanfare. Admittedly, up till now at least, the move from San Francisco to the mountains of Montana had been less eventful than he'd originally expected. So far, he had spent too many nights like this one, alone and isolated. Yesterday, Jack had decided to leave his mountain cabin and move to Missoula—a thriving metropolis by comparison. Yeah, well, first things first. He took another sip of coffee and struggled to stay awake and alert.

Reaching over to put the coffee back in the cup holder, Jack was suddenly blinded by bright light. Jerking up, trying to figure out what was happening, he heard the loud bellow of a logging truck's horn. He tensed on the wheel, fighting the urge to step on the brake with all his weight. He knew that doing so would probably roll the car. He craned his neck, staring hard into the oncoming headlights, looking around for somewhere to get out of the way. He couldn't see a thing. Though only a guardrail and a sheer drop bordered much of route 135, he turned to the right anyway, hoping for a shoulder.

The tires slid on gravel until the car came to a stop. Moments later, Jack was rocked in a wash of turbulence as the huge truck rumbled by, its horn soon receding in pitch and intensity. He released a white-knuckled grip on the wheel and sat for a few moments to let his hands stop shaking, then brushed his hair back and pulled onto the road once more.

Twenty minutes later, Jack rolled into the dirt parking lot in front of the mine. A teepee-like web of girders above the elevator shaft was darker than the early morning sky as he walked into the mine entrance. After putting his ID card into the security door, he got into the elevator and dialed the code for the fifty-first level, a mile below his feet. Express elevator straight to hell, he thought.

The cage shuddered and dropped as if the cable had just been cut. A nervous spasm tickled Jack's ribs before his stomach had a chance to catch up with the rest of his body. Once he had a chance to recover his equilibrium, he glanced through the elevator window at the shaft wall streaking by outside. Though he'd watched this spectacle a thousand times before, it never ceased to amaze him how all this rock was no more than a dirty pane of glass as far as neutrinos were concerned. After all this time, he still found it hard to fathom how a mile of rock only served to shield the detector from background noise, tuning out the constant static of cosmic rays produced by a torrent of particles forever raining onto the surface of the Earth. To the ghostly neutrino, the rock was all but invisible. If they'd done the experiment any closer to the surface, the whisper of neutrinos would have been drowned out by the thunder of everything else.

The cage rattled and rolled on its way down, giving Jack a vision of sparks flying from its rails. The thought snapped him to attention and set his adrenaline pumping. He couldn't help thinking about how dumb luck had presented him with this gold mine and a chance to hopscotch his way to scientific stardom. By determining the mass of the neutrino, a puzzle that had fueled speculation about the solution to the missing mass problem in the universe for years, his place in history would be assured. Why use an accelerator, he'd thought, when the sun was the perfect source. It brewed up a tremendous wind of neutrinos deep in its thermonuclear core. All he needed was a quiet detector to listen to what that wind was saying. The mine gave him the filter he needed. Other researchers before him had determined that neutrinos changed identity spontaneously between two different flavors as they traveled between the sun and Earth. Theoretically, at least, he knew that these oscillations only happened if neutrinos had mass, and if the masses of the two flavors were different. He brightened at the thought that they might already have enough data to see the effect.

The cage began to shake even more violently as it neared the bottom, sounding a high-pitched squeal, then abruptly grinding to a halt. Jack emerged and took a catwalk of planks over the muddy shaft floor, following a string of overhead incandescent bulbs to the lab airlock. Entering the control room, he was, as always, disoriented because of the darkness and clutter of equipment racks that lined the walls. He glanced at the partially open door on the far side of the room and noticed a sliver of light. As he crossed the floor, detector electronics hummed and clicked with eternal regularity.

"Melanie?"

No answer.

She probably couldn't hear him above the roar of the air conditioners. Mineshafts on the other side of the airlock were usually well over one hundred degrees and unbearably humid at this level, but the lab was cool and dry—the sensitive detector electronics didn't like heat. Though the project bosses could ignore the complaints of the staff, the complaints of the equipment were always taken seriously. He patted a cool metal console before pushing through the office door.

"Hey, anybody home?"

Jack watched as a young woman, sitting with her back to the door, shot to her feet, like a cat taken unawares by a loud noise.

Though he hadn't meant to scare her, Jack couldn't help cracking a smile. "Sorry," he offered lamely.

She looked flustered, eyes wide behind tortoiseshell rims, hand over her heart, short white lab coat still looking starched. The sight reaffirmed his preference for lab casual over bare midriffs and nose rings.

"You scared the hell outa me. For goodness sake, say something next time," she admonished.

"I did," replied Jack. "I thought there was an emergency." He was suddenly feeling put out by the apparent normalcy. Why had she gotten him up in the middle of the night anyway?

"Take a look at this," she urged, handing him a piece of paper.

He studied a graph on the paper. A series of bumps, some in approximate horizontal alignment, and others peaking or dipping below the ones to their left or right jumped out at him.

"What's this?" he asked. *Neutrino flavor as a function of time* was stenciled above the plot. She had turned things around on him; now she appeared amused and he felt off balance. Had she gotten him out here in the middle of the night for some half-baked practical joke? It didn't seem likely—not in character.

He took her in: hands on hips, a swash of hair dangling to the side of her horn rims, cocked stance on long slender legs—inviting him to question the graph. "You ran the neutrino flavors?"

"I wanted to see where we were, wanted to surprise you," she insisted.

"You surprised me alright." He picked up the paper and pursed his lips. "This can't be right—you know that, right?"

"I may know it, but tell the detector."

Before he could ask the obvious questions, she was ready with answers. "I moved the detector under the iron shelf, ran all the diagnostics with a radioactive source— there's nothing wrong."

Jack knew that partially blocking neutrinos by putting the detector under a mile of iron, then sending in a known signal, would flag any problems with the equipment. Melanie had dotted the i's and crossed the t's. Jack sat heavily; fatigue had set in with a vengeance. He tried to think, but this was so wrong that he didn't know where to start. "At a particular depth, we're supposed to see only one flavor," he said, trying to convince himself. Then something occurred to him—what a jerk. He smiled up at her.

"What?" she asked.

"These are just variations within errors," he stated confidently. "If I weren't so tired, I would have seen it right away."

"Fraid not," Melanie said, and handed him another plot, this one with error bars. She smiled wryly.

"Okay," he said, after glancing at the new plot. Clearing his mind, Jack struggled to take a fresh look. "Let's suppose this is for real. What does it mean?" His shoulders fell and he felt himself relax, making an effort not to think about his plummeting career.

He blinked, then shot her a look. "Taken as a whole, what does this remind you of?"

She stared blankly, Ivory Soap girl with a nerdy streak.

"You know what Morse code is, don't you?" he asked.

She lingered on the words, then laughed out loud. "What are you talking about?"

"No—just wait a minute. Give me a chance. I heard you out, now hear me out."

She sat on the desk—a little distracting—but he plowed ahead. He had her attention. "Morse code," he repeated.

"So you're saying what, this is a message?"

He saw a hint of sympathy in her eyes—perhaps reflecting an impression that he might be losing it. But he persisted. "The whole thing's unbelievable, so why not go all the way. If I forget about the science and just pretend I don't know where this came from, I'd say it looks like Morse code. Look at the spacing between peaks, see how some are close together and others are far apart?"

"Dots and dashes?"

"Yeah," he said, "dots and dashes."

"Jack, you're creeping me out." Melanie stood and rubbed her arms with nervous enthusiasm. After a moment, she said, "Okay, I'll bite. What's it say?"

Jack had to reach way back. True, he'd known Morse code as a kid, even had a short-wave radio, but that was a long time ago. Grabbing a blank piece of paper, he penciled out dots and dashes in concert with the graph. Once he had the code, he racked his memory for the corresponding letters and numbers, which he jotted down underneath the bumps and troughs on the original plot. When he was finished, he handed it to her.

"It's all numbers? You're sure?"

It was easy to read her mind; she was looking for words, evidence this wasn't all gibberish and they weren't chasing a wet dream. A random sequence of numbers could mean anything, including that there wasn't really anything in the signal.

"I know," he admitted, "I was hoping for more too."

Then he was struck by another thought. "Suppose *we* were sending a message like this." He noticed her skeptical smirk. "Just hear me out. Suppose we *could* send a message," he continued. "How long would it take for a detector like ours to receive enough data to form a character—statistically, I mean?"

"About two weeks," she said without hesitation, then paused. "Two weeks per dot or dash," she repeated, then started counting the characters. She looked up a little confounded. "This message would take about five months to send."

"Yeah. So if it took that long, wouldn't it make sense to make it as compact as possible?"

"Yes it would," she admitted, taking new interest in the string of numbers.

After a few long minutes, taking spaces into account, they were able to find a sequence they could both agree on: *135,6,23,530.*

"It's not a social security number," Jack pointed out, then noticed he was losing her again. Clearly, suspension of disbelief was taking its toll. She continued regarding him with obvious skepticism.

"What?" he asked.

"I don't know," she said. "How could someone send a message by neutrinos? They come from the sun, for pity's sake. Nobody can control the sun. And even if they could, who are these god-like people? Or better yet, where are they?"

Her shoulders slumped and Jack realized he'd taken it as far as he could. "We need a theorist," he declared.

Blowing a wisp of hair away, Melanie glanced at her watch. "Where are we going to get a theorist at 7 A.M.?"

"You had no trouble yanking me out of bed at 3 A.M. this morning—pretty rudely too," Jack complained.

* * *

In the early afternoon, with Melanie in tow, Jack rounded the corner into Barry Clay's office on the third floor of the Science Complex at the University of Montana. He'd known

Barry when they had both been grad students back in Berkeley. In the intervening years, Barry had become a respectable voice in particle theory, something that most of his friends had expected. Barry was always the go-to guy whenever Jack had gotten stuck on some fine point of a scientific paper. Jack had always considered Barry one of the more capable, if less famous young theorists, who had always been willing to give Jack the time of day.

Barry glanced up as they entered, his eyes instantly falling on Melanie. He gestured toward Jack. "You should've left him home. He makes a bad first impression." Then he stood and flashed a mouth full of pearly whites. "How've you been, man? Long time no hear."

Taking his massive outstretched hand, Jack concluded Barry hadn't changed much. His tank-top tee shirt displayed the biceps of a seasoned weight lifter, making it seem as if time had stood still for him. His close-cropped afro and smooth onyx skin made him look as young as when they'd been drinking buddies—frequenting the assorted lounges up and down Shattuck Avenue in Berkeley.

"So you still need help with your homework, eh?" Barry looked at Melanie, winked, then sat.

"Yeah, yeah," Jack said as he plopped the graphs down on Barry's desk. "Take a look at these, genius."

That got his attention. With the intensity that marked most good theorists, Barry drilled into the plots with total concentration. "Neutrino flavors?" he asked, still studying the papers in front of him. Finally, he looked up. "You know these are wrong—right?"

Melanie said, "I think they're right. I checked the detector, the electronics, and the software. I stand by these results."

"Hmmm," Barry exhaled and looked down at the graphs with renewed interest. To Jack's surprise, he seemed to be taking this more seriously than he'd expected. Did he really have some idea about what it meant?

"You're sure?" Barry asked, looking at Melanie again.

"Yes, I'm sure."

"I see," Barry said.

"See what?" Jack asked anxiously, as though waiting to learn whether he'd received a passing or failing grade.

Barry's gaze shifted between Jack and Melanie. "You guys understand quantum mechanics, right?"

"As well as your average experimentalist hack," Jack offered, "yeah."

"Okay, have you ever heard of the *Many Worlds* interpretation of quantum mechanics?" Barry asked.

"Are you serious?" Jack replied, starting to think that Barry was leading them down the garden path. "Come on, man, no jokes."

"I've heard of it," Melanie said. "It was a possible explanation of the double slit experiment proposed by Hugh Everett back in the late fifties. More an oddity than anything else, as far as I can tell."

Jack was amazed. Was he the only dummy in the room? "Just for the intellectually challenged, could you remind me of that little known piece of historical trivia?"

It was Melanie who spoke. "The double slit experiment describes what happens when you put a light source, a laser, for example, behind a screen with two holes in it. If you put a second screen in front of the first and turn the light on, you see a striped pattern on the second screen because of the interference between light waves from the two holes—like water waves when you drop two rocks close together into a pond."

"Yeah, I know," Jack said, a little impatient. As far as he was concerned, every schoolboy right out of diapers knew about the double slit experiment—so what?

"The interesting part comes when you dim the light," Barry said. "Imagine you turn the light down until there's only one particle of light at a time coming from the source. Remember, according to quantum mechanics, light has an interchangeable nature. It behaves like particles or waves interchangeably." He looked at his two students, both of whom seemed to be following the conversation. Barry continued. "So, a problem arises when you dim the light to one particle at a time and replace the second screen with a very sensitive photographic plate."

"If you wait awhile, then look at the plate, you find the same interference pattern," Melanie said.

"That's right," Barry said. "Each particle of light, each photon, leaves a dot on the film. After awhile, the dots add up to form the same light and dark bands in the original interference pattern."

"But how can that be?" Jack asked. "There's an interference pattern, but what did each individual photon interfere with?"

"That's the sixty-four thousand dollar question," Barry declared, jabbing a finger in Jack's direction. "Everett's explanation was that there are many parallel worlds involved in every quantum mechanics experiment. Every possible quantum outcome is realized in one of a multiplicity of other worlds while only one outcome is measured by experimenters in any given world."

Jack felt as if he were listening to a mystic, not a legitimate particle theorist. But he had to admit, he now remembered reading about the *Many Worlds* interpretation and knew that some credible scientists hadn't completely dismissed it out of hand.

"So what are you saying?" Jack asked.

"I'm saying that your neutrinos are like photons, and the flavors are actually an interference pattern. For example, flavor A could be a dark band while flavor B is a light band in the interference pattern. Now, if someone wanted to send a message, they might send it in a code, like Morse code"— Barry flashed a smile. "Yeah, you could change flavors by changing something akin to the distance between holes on the first screen. That distance gives you a sort of parallax, a depth perception by giving you an interference pattern whose dimensions correspond to the distance between holes. The separation between holes on the first screen changes the spacing of light and dark bands in the interference pattern."

"Wait a minute, wait a minute," Jack said. "You're losing me now."

"I know it's pretty thin, but bear with me here." Barry looked out the window, distracted, distant. "Suppose we had a roulette wheel," he said finally.

Jack grinned at Melanie. "Now that's the Barry I know." He noticed she wasn't smiling back. She'd taken off her glasses and was staring at Barry in an eerie way that gave him a chill. He'd never seen her like this before. Her gray-green eyes were luminous with intensity. Jack sat back and let Barry run with it.

"Suppose this roulette wheel had a bunch of red and black slots. Each pair of red and black slots had the same number, like red seven and black seven, and red eight and black eight—you know?"

Jack watched Melanie nod. She was giving him the creeps.

"Now, suppose each number is a different universe, and each color a different outcome to the same experiment being performed in all those numbered worlds. When we spin the wheel and put the ball down, it bumps into all the different slots and bounces around. That's like our neutrinos interfering with all those other universes. The roulette wheel, as a whole, is like quantum mechanics reaching out and touching all those ghostly parallel worlds. When the ball stops on a particular color, it's like one of the flavors on your graph."

Everyone was silent, then Melanie asked, "How does that person in the other universe send a particular flavor, you know, send a dot or dash of Morse code?"

"I don't know," Barry said. "Maybe move their detector under a barrier, a screen that's significantly more dense than the rock above yours."

"The iron shelf," Melanie whispered. Jack glanced at Barry and explained. "There's a deep stratum of iron ore almost the full mile above the White Cloud mine. We have the detector on rails and can put it under the shelf to determine the relative proportion of flavors."

Barry bored into the plots once more. "Can I hold onto these for awhile?" he asked, not looking up. He continued studying the papers, occasionally jotting down mathematical calculations in the margins.

Deciding that they'd probably gotten as much from Barry as he was willing to give, Jack and Melanie left him in his office, pondering the mysteries of the universe, and drove back to White Cloud in silence.

* * *

Jack watched as Melanie got out of the car and walked back to the mine entrance. She'd barely said goodbye—thanks for the ride. And she hadn't said so much as a word during the ride back to the mine. He shook his head, disappointed by her blank dismissal, and started back to his cabin. It had been a long day, confusing, and confounding. The prospect of catching up on his lost night's sleep seemed like an idea whose time had come. He'd think about the message later, when his mind had a chance to clear.

He wound up the familiar mountain road and happened to linger on the route 135 sign. Something about it made him tingle. The shield-like shape of the sign reminded him of a police badge. The bold black font of the numbers—something about it was off. Then he looked down and noticed the clock on the dash—5:30. "Five-thirty," he mumbled to himself. "One-thirty-five—five-thirty."

Before he knew it, he let up on the accelerator and pulled off the road. When the car came to a stop, he just sat there with the motor running, seized by a strange feeling that he'd been here before. He was brought back to the present by an ear-piercing screech of tires, followed by a shrill scraping sound. He looked farther up the road, toward a high bend, and saw a logging truck.

"Oh shit," Jack whispered, as he frantically reached for the door. His hand, clammy and sweaty, slipped on the handle as he clawed to push it down. Turning to look out the window, he saw the truck come barreling around the corner, skid on some dirt or something, and jackknife. Flipping over, it was now sliding sideways, raising a rain of sparks around its gas tanks as it continued heading directly toward him.

Feeling the handle depress, Jack pushed the door wide open, slid across the passenger's seat, and launched himself through the door and down an embankment. Suddenly, he was hurdling down a steep slope, grabbing at shrubbery and backpedaling with his heels, trying to slow himself. At last he felt a patch of loose soil, dug in, and managed to stop. Glancing down, he saw the tops of tall trees over the lip of a considerable drop no more than ten feet in front of him.

With blood pounding in his ears, he heard the concussive sound of the truck explode, followed by a small earthquake. Taking a deep breath, he smelled gasoline and burning tires as he propped himself up, turned, and saw black smoke darkening the cloudless blue sky. Jack jabbed a hand into his pocket, recovered his cell phone, and dialed 911. Once he'd reported the accident, he lowered the phone and ignored the tinny voice of the operator asking who he was.

When he'd made his way up and over the embankment again, he found his car was still there, motor idling, just as he'd left it. There wasn't so much as a scratch on it. The scene on 135 was another matter. Debris littered the road, most of it burning. The truck was unrecognizable, and he was sure the driver hadn't survived. One-thirty-five—five-thirty, the numbers seemed to repeat in his head like a looping tape. Then he remembered, today was June twenty-third—
135,6,23,530.

* * *

Jack sat on his porch. He'd been home for a couple of hours when he saw Melanie's Toyota coming up the driveway, raising a cloud of red dust in its wake. She got out, climbed the porch stairs, and then sat cross-legged in front of him as he drank the last of the bourbon in his tumbler.

"You all right?" she asked finally.

"One-thirty-five, six, twenty-three, five-thirty—you sent that message, didn't you?" Jack asked.

Melanie continued regarding him stoically. She placed her elbows on her knees and cupped her chin in both hands. "How could I have sent that message? I called you, remember? You're the one who thought it was Morse code, not me."

"I don't mean you specifically," Jack said. "I mean the other you." He made a grand gesture with his arms as though encompassing some unknown, unseen, reality.

"How am I supposed to know that?" she asked.

"I saw the way you looked at Barry this afternoon when he explained this thing, something happened—something clicked. You felt something, didn't you?"

"Maybe," Melanie admitted. "Maybe."

Her horned rimmed glasses seemed out of place. They were a look that he associated with the mineshaft—the studious Melanie. It dawned on him that she must have gotten the news and just rushed out here, barely taking time to lose the lab coat.

"What about the time thing?" he asked.

"What do you mean?"

"You know. By the time the other you in that other quantum universe sent the message, the other me was dead."

"It may not work like that," Melanie said. Jack sensed a certain strength in the declaration and found it somehow comforting.

"Barry's roulette wheel appears to span our space as well as other dimensional boundaries," Melanie said. "Quantum mechanics is non-local. It seems to have transactions that encompass a region of space-time rather than being tied to a particular place. By the same token, it may also be non-local in time. Maybe there are many copies of us out there." She repeated Jack's grand gesture with her arms. "Maybe some of our copies have branched off in a variety of ways and over a span of time. The other Melanie must have realized that," she said.

"What about the fact that if we hadn't received the message, I would never have been a bowling pin for that logging truck today," Jack said.

"Think about it," Melanie said. "You usually go home around that time. What difference does it make whether we spent the day wondering about the message, or just doing what we usually do. Chances are, you would have been on 135 at about 5:30 anyway, message or no message."

Jack supposed that if those other dimensions really existed, his relationship with the other Melanie must be qualitatively different. A relationship that the ghostly Melanie had gone to great lengths to preserve, if not for her, for some sisterly copy she was convinced inhabited another quantum roulette slot in the inscrutable labyrinth of space-time. He imagined the other Melanie moving the detector in and out of the iron shelf, day after day, for weeks and months on end, painstakingly carving out dots and dashes in hopes that their copies might get the message in time—and understand it.

"Why'd you do it?" Jack asked. "It must have taken an incredible effort, not to mention an unbelievable leap of faith."

Melanie flushed; he'd hit a nerve. Even if their copies throughout the quantum realm were different, Jack assumed there must be an underlying sameness that unified the whole structure. It was this belief that had led him to suspect that his Melanie understood her twin's motivations, even though they were separated by an unassailable quantum barrier.

She glanced up at him quizzically, then slowly showed a steely resolve that he'd never seen before. It was as if she'd come to a decision, a fork in the road that she'd suddenly decided to take.

"So, you're going to drink your dinner tonight, is that right?" she asked, noting the empty tumbler in his hand.

Her expression was disarmingly warm, reflecting a familiarity that they'd never really had, not in this life anyway. For the first time tonight, Jack was at a loss for words as he spun the tumbler in his fingers.

"It's been a long day. Why don't we get something to eat?" Melanie suggested. "Want to take me to dinner?"

She took her glasses off. He'd always found her attractive, but now she seemed appealing in a way that their edgy relationship had previously never allowed.

Jack just stared at her. He felt the draw, but this was all very confusing.

"Do you want to take me out?" Melanie repeated.

"Ah, okay," Jack blurted—then blushed and felt self-conscious. He'd said yes too fast, like a little puppy licking her wrist. Was he being swept up in some cosmic dance that he was only dimly aware of? Was there some larger organiz-

ing principle at work here—something that could reach beyond whatever barrier separated quantum universes into the
lives of people inhabiting such disparate worlds?

Melanie got to her feet and started off the porch. Then
she stopped and turned. "Oh—by the way—I'm driving this
time," she said, smiling.

Jack returned the smile, then followed her to the car.

The End

Book Three: One Way Ticket

"There once was a woman named Bright
Who traveled much faster than light:
She set out one day
In a relative way,
And returned on the previous night."
— Anonymous

One Way Ticket

Joshua Bernstein watched the stars burning like luminous crystals in a glass of dark liquid. He had discovered the observation deck shortly after the *Hera* had left Earth orbit as it streaked into deep space above the plane of the elliptic toward the Oort Cloud, which lay a light-year beyond the Sun. Apparently, this artifact of the early solar system's formation was the source of comets he had seen arcing across the sky above his home in Seattle, a home he feared he might never see again. Joshua knew very little about space travel outside the solar system. Though he often traveled between the planets for his job, this was something different. Earthly ships were not capable of carrying passengers into interstellar space, which was still the province of experimental probes. But then the *Hera* was not an Earthly craft—the thought was intimidating. He imagined that the details of this voyage were probably of great interest to many of his former colleagues, but of little interest to him. On the contrary, he was more concerned with the past than the present or future. As he looked at the star-laden void in front of the ship, all he could see were nondescript points of light that seemed eternal and intrinsically separate from the human sphere. Perhaps if he knew more about them, they wouldn't be as irrelevant as they seemed.

New Horizons, a government agency, had overseen the preparations for the trip. The agency was originally founded at the request of the Spacers, a branch of humanity that had left for deep space centuries before. Not much was known about them now except that they had agreed to provide conveyance to the stars for certain human ventures. Part of the reason that Joshua had decided to come on this journey was to meet Spacers. But he had been disappointed to learn that the Spacer crew of the *Hera* was segregated on decks of the ship inaccessible to the passengers. Members of the human staff of New Horizons, who had disembarked before the ship had left orbit, had made all of the arrangements, and apparently, the ship was fully automated. In fact, he had not seen a single Spacer.

After departure, Joshua had spent his first few days on the ship walking the corridors of the passenger's deck. It was a big ship, filling the windows of the shuttle as they had approached the *Hera* high above Earth, before boarding. The corridors were round and smooth, with a composite floor that gave underfoot, and diffuse lighting that was everywhere, but seemed to come from nowhere. The thing that fascinated him the most, though, were the many terrariums that were set in recesses along the walls, like some museum exhibit that extended for what seemed like miles along the twisting, turning paths that threaded the passenger's deck. Unlike a museum, these exhibits were real. They were mostly of desert plants: palms, ferns, and perennials, set in reddish, sandy soil that reminded him of the type of landscapes he'd seen on treks through canyons on Mars. But unlike the hardier, genetically bred species that now adorned the terraformed, man-made Martian canyons, these plants were rare, if not extinct. He remembered seeing their likeness in videos of ancient Mars, when there were still domed cities, before the bio-holocaust on Earth in the early twenty-fifth century. Joshua would occasionally kneel next to an exhibit and run his hands through the dirt, feel its coarse grains, then raise it to his nose and smell its ancient, dusty aroma, which conjured up visions of a civilization long past.

Although the accommodations were comfortable, he was lonely. Joshua rarely saw anyone else, either on his treks, or as the result of visitors to his quarters—of which there'd been none. After boarding the ship, there was a brief orientation by a representative of New Horizons; and following that, there'd been a get-acquainted reception, but none of it stuck. Most of the passengers had retreated to their respective social circles. More than likely, this was not their first interstellar flight. Extended, deep space travel was the province of a hard pioneering class with few ties to the normal ebbs and flows of planetary society. And since Joshua was an academic, he remained the odd man out.

The only time that Joshua had extended contact with anyone else was at dinner, which was the only scheduled meal. He was told that he could drop by the cafeteria any time of the day or night, but dinner was between 6PM and 8PM Earth standard time each evening. He suspected that this had been planned as a way of facilitating bonding among the passengers. Only in his case, it hadn't worked.

* * *

After a vigorous trek through the corridors, Joshua decided to head to the observation lounge to relax. But as soon as he approached the lounge bulkhead, he began to feel hunger pangs. He checked his watch and realized it was 6:30 PM. If he didn't start for the cafeteria now, he might miss dinner.

When he'd filled his tray with soy-steak, mashed sweet potato, a green salad, and a glass of wheat beer, he turned and surveyed the dinning room. There were several large tables at which men and women were talking, laughing, drinking, and eating. He noticed one table across the room where he recognized some people—and there was an empty chair. When he sat down, a couple of people stopped eating momentarily, others paused their conversations and gave him a nod. Once he got settled, things continued as before.

"We've been out from Earth for a month, and I haven't seen a ghost yet," Mugabe said. He was a stout, leather-skinned man across the table.

"Ghosts only come out at night," a woman next to him said, and smiled wryly.

"This is my third trip on a Spacer ship; I've only seen them at the end of a trip, when we're offloading. And even then, it was only from far away," Harris said.

Harris was one of the few on board with whom he had ever had anything approaching an extended conversation. Harris was a capable looking man with broad shoulders and dark, deep-set eyes in an ebony, sharply sculpted face. From their conversations, Joshua guessed that Harris was well educated. The man certainly had an impressive detailed knowledge of history.

The woman that had made the crack about ghosts coming out at night stared at Joshua as Harris spoke. She had a curious twinkle in her blue eyes that made Joshua want to smile too.

"Harris tells me you're an anthropologist," the woman said. She had never stopped looking at him, elbows planted on the table, hands knitted together in a steeple on which she rested her sharp chin.

She had caught him with a big piece of steak in his mouth. Joshua chewed and swallowed hastily. "Yeah, that's right," was all he could manage, as he tried to stifle a choking cough.

"What the hell could an anthropologist want by coming way out here?" a man to his left gibed.

"What are any of us doing out here?" another woman asked.

"We're makin' money," the man said. "At least some of us are." The man winked at the woman who had made the comment.

"There was an extraterrestrial intelligent species found on *Cor Caroli*," Joshua said. "I study cultures. "Up till now, no other extraterrestrial culture has ever been found."

"You mean the kangaroos?" the man said. "I've seen the videos back from *Cor Caroli*, you could just as well have gone to the zoo instead of crossing a hundred light years of space."

There were laughs from a few people around the table, others just smirked and looked down at their plates.

Joshua had expected as much. He smiled. "Maybe I'll write a book about it when I get back—make a good chunk of change." He winked at the man, who was taking him more seriously all of a sudden.

The woman with the blue eyes laughed, "If you're interested in extraterrestrial life, why not study the ghosts?"

"The ghosts?" Joshua asked.

"Our hosts," the woman said.

"She means the Spacers," Harris said.

"It's not like I haven't tried," Joshua complained. "I've sent many requests to New Horizons for interviews over the years—they're not interested. Oh, there are always reasons, they try to be polite, but they're not really interested in talking. Not to me at least."

"Those sons-of-bitches aren't interested in any of us," the man said. He looked around the room, scowling. "And I don't care if they hear me," he added defiantly.

"They don't like us, but they ferry us all over the universe, all expenses paid," Harris said. "How do you explain that?"

There was an uncomfortable silence. Most of these people were more familiar with the frontier than with the secure lives that planetary populations enjoyed. They were used to being independent and in control, Joshua thought. The idea that they were now in interstellar space, out of reach of any human technology, and under the watchful eyes of aliens who would not even speak to them, left everyone a little ill at ease. They'd known this all along, but to be reminded of it out loud was unsettling.

"You're an anthropologist, do you know anything about the ghosts?" the blue-eyed woman asked. She was no longer smiling.

Joshua took a breath; everyone was looking at him now. "They're not aliens."

"They're not human," the man across the table said.

"Not anymore," Joshua said. "I'll grant you that."

"If not aliens," the blue-eyed woman asked, "then who are they?"

Joshua noticed that everything at the table had stopped—they were all looking at him. He took a breath. "Most of what we know about them is from documents from before the bio-holocaust."

"But that was a thousand years ago," Mugabe said. "Even though much of the infrastructure on Earth was left intact, things fell apart without maintenance. Almost all the people on Earth were gone. Those that survived were mostly sick and soon they were turning on each other. A hundred years after the bio-war, almost everything was lost—Earth was a dead planet. So how can you be so sure that Spacers are human?"

There was a cynical, humorless grin on the man's rough face. His description of the dark ages had clearly taken the mood down a couple of notches.

"That's right," Joshua agreed. "But the original Spacers didn't come from Earth, they came from Mars. Although the collapse of Earth was hard on Mars, Martian society remained viable and actually prospered. Their electronic records remained intact."

"So who are our hosts?" Harris asked.

Joshua noticed that unlike the others at the table, Harris had continued to eat. He'd taken an occasional pull on his beer and seemed to be enjoying this. His question seemed more of an entree for Joshua to continue than anything else.

"Well, it's believed that they are the descendants of a small group of bio-engineered children that escaped on one of Earth's first starships about a hundred years before the bio-wars."

"You mean designer people, like the ones on pre-holocaust Earth?" the blue-eyed woman asked.

"No. These were very special children, genetically rede-signed almost from scratch by an Earth expatriate and a Martian geneticist. The whole thing is sketchy, but they somehow escaped on one of the first RamScoop starships to Procyon, a star about ten light years from Earth. Accounts are kind of confused because all this took place just before the Martian wars of secession."

The man across the table started laughing. "Are you sure you didn't dream this up?"

Joshua smiled, "You asked."

There was another silence, then Harris asked, "So why are they doing this?"

"Doing what?"

"Ferrying us around out of the goodness of their hearts, even if they don't think enough of us to talk to us?"

Joshua took a drink. "I think they feel kinship—maybe a sense of obligation."

"If they're so charitable, then why don't they teach us how to build our own ships?" Harris asked, a little more engaged now.

"Think about it," Joshua said. "We almost made ourselves extinct a thousand years ago. A hundred years before that, we drove their ancestors into space. After the war, they came back and saved us from the Stone Age. For the last thousand years, we've managed to wage several other pointless wars. Would you arm people like that with this kind of technology?"

Harris exhaled a muffled laugh, shook his head, then got up and left. One by one the others followed suit. Joshua sat at the empty table, finished his beer, then left an empty dinning room.

* * *

Each day, as Joshua returned to the acceleration lounge on the observation deck, the scene became more bizarre than the day before. The star field seemed to be slowly drawing into a clump at the center of the monitor. At first, the effect had been so subtle that he'd scarcely noticed. But after a week, the change was unmistakable.

He asked Harris about it. "What's wrong with this picture?"

Harris stared into a soap bubble thin screen, absently stroking his well-manicured black goatee. "It looks completely fine."

"Where are the stars going?" Joshua asked, tracing his finger through the conspicuous black on the outer edges of the starscape.

Harris grinned, "First time in deep space, eh?"

Joshua shrugged, trying to dispel his obvious inexperience, a perception that could only diminish his standing among the passengers. He felt cold as the sweat on his brow evaporated in the draft of the air conditioning. Adding to his discomfort, Harris's condescending grin was beginning to annoy him.

"It's a relativistic effect, a visual aberration," Harris said. "We're going fast now, probably eighty or ninety percent the speed of light. The faster we go, the more everything in front of us collapses into the forward part of our field of view."

"I knew that," Joshua said. He felt like a fool.

Harris barked a quick laugh, "Give it another month and a half, everything around the ship will be right about here." He made a small circle around the center of the screen with his finger. "That's when all the fun starts." Then, with a dismissive turn that signaled he had better things to do, Harris left the observation deck.

Joshua spent the next month and a half alone most of the time. On occasion, he'd see Harris or Mugabe in the corridors, or in one of the common areas on the passenger's floor, but the other men made him feel like an outsider, so he mostly kept to himself. He developed a daily routine to stave off the growing sense that he'd made a terrible mistake accepting this mission. True, they had made him feel important for a time, but now that time was up, and the bill had come due. It slowly dawned on him that far from being a position of honor, or a commission that most people would covet, this was a job that could only be done by someone like him, a chronic outsider. He had scant little to look back on, and nothing much to look forward to—no family, and not many friends. Harris and Mugabe must have sensed it and slowly withdrew.

As part of his daily routine, he spent the hour after lunch on the observation deck. Though at first the stars had meant little to him, his personal loneliness had soon sparked an appreciation of their desolate beauty. He became enthralled with the three-dimensional view of the star-cluttered void, a tangle of pinprick points strewn in a chaotic vista that made him feel as if he were falling. He began to see more detail, the hint of color in some of them, the wispy smears of colored gas in the backgrounds of others. But just as Harris had said, the panorama had continued to recede. Now all that was left was an amorphous white smear at the center of the screen. Disappointing, Joshua thought. Even this had been taken from him. He rose sullenly and turned to leave, but stopped in mid stride, startled by the creature that had come up behind him.

The woman, if you could call her that, was as quiet as a cat. She had snuck up on him in the stone silence of the deck without so much as the sound of a footstep on the hard composite floor. Joshua couldn't help staring. She was unnaturally pale, almost an albino, with so little melanin in her skin that it looked to be made of porcelain. Under platinum hair, she appeared to be little more than a parody of a flesh and blood woman. But in her dark almond eyes, Joshua found the kernel of her being. They reflected depth in a face that otherwise exuded all the warmth of a mannequin. She was a Spacer, one of the seldom seen crew, part of the human race that had all but abandoned living on planets hundreds of years before, opting instead to run between the stars in ships like the *Hera*.

After a long uncomfortable silence, Joshua said, "Can I help you?"

Unblinking eyes stared back at him; a hint of a smile stretched across delicate pink lips. "That's what I was going to ask you, Mr. Bernstein."

"Help me? Help me with what?"

The Spacer glanced at the monitor, focusing in on the clump of stars at its center. "We'll be tunneling soon. Have you ever tunneled before, Mr. Bernstein?"

The question caught him off guard. "I was told it was safe."

"Safety is not the issue," the woman said.

"I'm sorry, I didn't get you name, miss. . ."

"Virginia," the woman said.

"Virginia," Joshua echoed. It made him think of green fields under a hazy southern sun, something out of antiquity, not some bizarre synthetic imitation of a woman.

Virginia was watching him. She cocked her head slightly, as if trying to fathom the odd expression that had co-opted his features at the mention of her name.

"They told you that you wouldn't be coming back, didn't they?" Virginia asked.

"What do you mean?" Joshua said. "Once we're finished on *Cor Caroli*, I expect to return to Earth."

Yes, of course," Virginia said. "But not the same Earth, you understand that, don't you, Mr. Bernstein?"

Joshua could only stare at her; where was she going with all this?

"Won't you sit?" Virginia made a hand motion toward the couch.

Joshua reluctantly lowered himself into the acceleration lounge. Virginia sat next to him. The seat expanded and molded itself to accommodate their combined contours like thick gelatin.

"Do you understand the conditions imposed by a trip to a destination as distant as *Cor Caroli*, Mr. Bernstein?"

"I know it will take a long time as seen on Earth."

"Yes, a long time," Virginia said. "During this last month on the ship, twenty years have passed on Earth. Many of the people you knew are now middle aged. Your parents may have died."

"My parents were dead when we left," Joshua said. A slight nausea tightened the pit of his stomach.

Virginia continued staring at him. He had no idea what a creature like this might be thinking; it was unnerving.

Virginia said, "Without tunneling, it would take another two hundred and forty Earth years to get to *Cor Caroli* at our present speed, and, if we just turned around and came back, almost five hundred years will have passed by the time we return to Earth. But, over such a long time, it would not be the same Earth."

"But we can tunnel," Joshua declared.

"Yes," Virginia said. "We can tunnel, and that will cut the time down to approximately forty years. But you see, Mr. Bernstein, when and if you do return, things will be different."

Virginia paused and glanced at the monitor. The stars were a compressed bright mass at the center of the screen surrounded by a thick halo of deep black that looked eerily empty.

"Take my hands, Mr. Bernstein," Virginia said urgently.

Before he could react, the creature grabbed his hands in a quick smooth motion and held them painfully tight. He tried to pull back, but Virginia held him in a vise-like grip that he couldn't even loosen. Joshua raised his eyes in submission and moaned a muted whimper. Suddenly, he felt incredibly dizzy, then lurched forward in slow motion.

"What's. . ." He tried to speak, but couldn't. It was as though he hadn't enough strength to work his mouth. The meager effort made him tired. Something was sapping his endurance; something was deathly wrong—but what?

Joshua panned the room in a drunken daze. He'd felt this way once before when he'd run so hard that he'd almost blacked out. But blackout wasn't the right word for this; it was more like a whiteout. He was on the edge, a precarious balance between consciousness and unconsciousness. The objects in the room looked like two-dimensional watermarks without sufficient contrast to make them appear real. All that remained to anchor him to the world were those dark almond eyes. Virginia had loosened her hold on him and was now rubbing the outer part of his hands with her thumbs. His hands appeared as bleached as hers, making it hard to tell them apart. Aberrant thoughts were flooding into his head; visions of grand things, which he'd never known, were bursting into his mind in a kaleidoscope of experience. He reveled in the awesome power of a fast-spinning pulsar from a god-like vantage that permitted him to feel its sweeping magnetic fields like a strong gale. Then he was suspended in the photosphere of a brown dwarf star as it slowly consumed the remainder of its nuclear fuel, in the death throws of its life, which had stretched many billions of years.

After an indefinite time, Joshua slowly started regaining his senses. Things were becoming better defined, as if taking on mass, reasserting their reality from a shadowy land of dreamy visions. His hands lay limp on Virginia's outstretched palms. She was smiling at him with warmth that seemed incongruous with her doll-white mannequin face.

"What's wrong with me?" Joshua rasped. He put an open hand on his damp forehead.

Virginia glanced in the direction of the monitor, "Look, Mr. Bernstein."

Joshua saw a bight yellow star at the center of a magnificent stellar backdrop, which spread over the void with less distortion now. "What's that star?" Joshua asked.

"*Cor Caroli.* We're braking now and should be there in a little over a month, ship time," Virginia said, placing his hand gently on his lap.

"But how can that be? It's a hundred and thirty light years away. We've been traveling for just a few months."

Then looking around the room, Joshua said, "I thought we were going to tunnel."

"While I've been holding your hands, we've shunted over a hundred light years of the continuum, Mr. Bernstein. We did tunnel. Perhaps you felt it, a disorientation?"

"But what's happened? Why do I feel so strange?"

"Do you understand what tunneling is, Mr. Bernstein?"

Joshua stared at her, unsure of himself, realizing how little he understood about anything that was happening.

"Tunneling is a process that is typically associated with quantum objects, like subatomic particles. In the macroscopic world, the world we're conscious of, it doesn't happen."

"But how?"

Virginia smiled. "The *Hera* rapidly changes the vacuum polarization of space, which induces a kind of asymmetric vacuum depletion, or Casimir region around the ship. We use this field for propulsion. It is a kind of antigravity."

"But how?"

"There is another effect of the Casimir field. We can momentarily induce everything within the field into a single, multi-particle, quantum state. And if we're close enough to the speed of light when we do, we can quantum tunnel through the scalar potential that supports space itself. What you felt during the transition, while I held your hands, Mr. Bernstein, was our sharing of a single quantum state. During that moment, we were the same thing—in the same place."

She rose smoothly and smiled down at him. He didn't want her to leave. It was as though a part of him had just peeled off. The thought of her sudden absence made him want to reach out for her, but instead he forced his hands into fists and pressed them hard against his thighs.

"I have to go," Virginia said, and moved to the door.

"Will I see you again?" Joshua called out.

She hung at the door for a moment, her back to him, then left the observation deck without a sound.

* * *

It was a balmy day; the air was thick with the rich scents of vegetation after a warm rain. Dense white clouds hung in a gunmetal gray sky as Joshua watched the shuttle hover above the tarmac and then slowly rise under the deafening roar of its thrusters. By and by the sound reached a crescendo, then diminished as the shuttle disappeared into the haze. Soon, Joshua heard only the mocking calls of alien animals in a forest of large rhubarb-like trees, their blood red fibrous trunks sprawling into a mass of crooked branches supporting a canopy of dark green leaves.

"Sir, your bags?"

The low raspy voice startled him. Joshua lowered his gaze to find a Carolian standing in front of him, its four long fingers extended from a double-jointed palm. The creature's large gray eyes were the color of the sky, giving the momentary impression that he was staring right through the thing's head.

"Uh, my bags—I can take them," Joshua said. He bent down to grab them, then stopped, and rose again.

"I'm sorry, I'm Joshua Bernstein; I'm glad to meet you." Joshua stuck out a shaky hand, not quite meeting the scaly palm of the Carolian.

The creature stood, looking at him, leaning slightly backward on its stubby tail, which was planted on the ground

behind it like an upside down hook. It stared at Joshua's outstretched hand a moment, then bent down, hoisted the bags,
turned, and started a slow kangaroo-like lope toward the car
where Harris and Mugabe were already talking to their hosts.

In a moment, Joshua joined them. "You must be Dr.
Bernstein," a brawny outdoorsman said, as he pumped Joshua's hand. "I'm Christian Azise, Governor of New California,
and this is my wife, Irene."

Azise's wife was an apt compliment to the macho Governor, with an athletic build, curves in all the right places, and
a healthy flash of sweat accentuating ample cleavage under a
barely buttoned shirt.

Harris stood there smirking, watching Joshua cringe under the man's iron handshake. Finally, Azise gave a grateful
Joshua his hand back and continued beaming, as if the small
band of Earthers was nothing short of the *Second Coming*.

"Mista Bernstein," Irene said, with a coy smile stretched
across full lips, which Joshua found stimulating and scary all
at the same time.

Soon they were driving frighteningly fast down a dirt
road with the Carolian at the wheel, leaving a long trail of
reddish-brown dust behind what Azise called an SUV. The
primitive vehicle stank of fossil fuel emissions, something
unknown on Earth for hundreds of years. This whole weird
encounter was like being transported back in time, which
was, the more Joshua thought about it, exactly what it was.

The Carolian drove in anonymity, never introduced,
never even acknowledged. Joshua found it hard to understand. As far as anyone on Earth knew, *Cor Caroli Alpha
Four* was the only planet where life had ever been found, and
intelligent life at that. After the discovery of tunneling, long

voyages in Spacer starships were actually faster than messages between the stars; so if another life-bearing planet had been found in the meantime, word hadn't filtered back to Earth yet. As far as Joshua was concerned, the discovery of sentient extraterrestrial life had been the greatest single event in human history. But here, apparently, Carolians were treated little better than dogs.

"Racing good luck that you decided to come, Mista Bernstein," Azise was saying. "Why, after the discovery of the Artifact last year, a state-of-the-art archeologist is exactly what we need."

Joshua sat up. "The Artifact?"

"You didn't know?" Irene said, leaning forward, her charms way out in front.

"Uh, no," Joshua admitted. "I came here to study the Carolian culture." He looked around at his hosts, their blank stares making him ill at ease.

"Culture?" Azise asked. "The Carolians are little more than animals."

Irene was nodding in solidarity.

Joshua glanced at the front seat. "I wasn't aware that animals could drive, as well as speak and write."

The Governor glared at Joshua with obvious disapproval. Irene said, "I thought you received our message about the Artifact."

"Fraid not," Harris said. The man had been uncharacteristically silent up till now. Probably enjoying my discomfort, Joshua thought.

"Tunneling's fast, but it's not that fast," Harris said. He turned back to the Governor. "Now what about that Artifact?"

"Bout a year ago, a couple of farmers digging around an old Carolian village found it," Azise said.

"Yup, they found it," Irene agreed.

"A metal cylinder about a meter long." Azise made an expansive gesture with his heavily muscled arms, showing how big it was. "Strange thing though, we can't open it, don't even know what it's made of either."

"Got some strange writing on it too," Irene said.

"Carolian writing?" Joshua asked. He was sitting way forward now, all his reservations about coming to *Cor Caroli* long gone. This was nothing short of the opportunity of a lifetime, and he had just stumbled into it.

"Sort of," Azise admitted. "But not quite the same. No way the slugs could have made that thing."

"Slugs?" Joshua asked.

Harris gave him a sharp surreptitious elbow to the side. Azise and his wife ignored the question. The Carolian kept driving, a virtual non-entity, deaf and dumb by force of habit.

They continued in a cloud of dust over expansive dirt roads that snaked through a valley bordered on the north by azure-gray mountains that melted into a gray-green sky. Joshua sat back and tried to absorb what had happened on *Cor Caroli* since the last Earth ship had come and gone more than a hundred years before. He didn't know a lot about official settlement policy, especially policy that included previsions for intelligent indigenous life, perhaps because intelligent life had never been found before. In fact, the circumstances of interstellar travel to planets as distant as *Cor Caroli* guaranteed that if anything unusual were ever found, word of the discovery back on Earth would lag the event by at least fifty years. But it was pretty obvious that something unforeseen had happened here. The settlers, instead of making suitable arrangements with the natives, had obviously taken over the planet.

From the back seat of the car, Joshua could see long stretches of cultivated fields on both sides of the road. Through the warm mists, which rose up from the dark rich soil, he could see row after endless row of wheat-like crops, their golden stalks and fuzzy arching limbs forming a sea of shimmering shoots in the afternoon breeze. Among the rows, Joshua noticed Carolians hard at work, either picking something, or just tending the plants. They bobbed above the golden hedges, beneath straw hats, as they hopped about, doing whatever it was they were doing under the watchful eye of an occasional settler. Joshua found the scene more disappointing than shocking, more familiar than unexpected. His fellow humans had come a staggering distance across the void, but had progressed a surprisingly short distance in overcoming their own societal weaknesses.

Eventually, they came to a large house on the outskirts of a settlement of red brick buildings, perhaps the Governor's mansion, Joshua thought. After an unceremonious meal, the Carolian driver was instructed to show him to his room. Joshua followed the creature as it carried his bags, with slow heavy steps, up a winding staircase to the second floor. The Carolian made its way down a plaster hallway adorned in alabaster designs, opened a red-wood door, then placed his bags at the foot of an antique four-poster bed. As he passed to leave, Joshua reached out and caught him by the sleeve, then quickly let go. The Carolian paused, glanced down at his arm where Joshua had touched him, then stared at Joshua in an inscrutable way that conveyed an air of bewilderment.

"Please," Joshua managed. "Please, can I speak to you a moment?"

"Why?" the creature asked, its flat face devoid of emotion, its large oval eyes unblinking.

"Because I don't know what's happening here," Joshua said.

The creature cocked its head. "Why?" it asked.

"Because there's something wrong here; it's not supposed to work like this."

The creature just stared. In the ponderous silence, Joshua realized there was some kind of singing in the distance, something filtering in through the partially open bedroom window. Pulling the drapes aside, he saw the ghostly orange glow of a campfire reflected in the distant trees. A low melodic chant was coming from the direction of the fire, something reminiscent of a tribal ceremony. He thought there might be instruments, drums maybe, but he wasn't sure.

He turned back to the Carolian, who was watching him closely now.

"What's that?" Joshua asked.

The Carolian emitted a series of clicks, punctuating a lyrical language, which Joshua assumed was its native tongue. "We ask our gods to take Earthmen away." It glanced at the door, then back at Joshua. "Earthmen bad, make *Twie-Twie Tanonga* bad since I was small."

"*Twie-Twie Tanonga?*" Joshua asked.

"*Twie-Twie Tanonga,*" the creature repeated, as if talking to a dunce. "You call, *Cor Caroli.*"

"Not all Earthmen are bad," Joshua whispered unconvincingly. "It's not supposed to be like this."

"It is this way—long as I remember," the creature said. "I know what I see."

It started for the door.

"Wait," Joshua called. "Do you have a name?"

Its slit of a mouth seemed to contort into something resembling amusement. It was the first time that Joshua had seen any expression at all on its tan, scaled face. He had come to believe that Carolians didn't have the facial muscles necessary to show expression in the same way humans did, but he'd be damned if that wasn't a smile.

"Onda," the creature said, then it turned and left the room.

* * *

Joshua tossed and turned, trying to get to sleep. It was a comfortable bed, more familiar and inviting than anything he'd experienced on the Hera, but he just couldn't get the creature's sardonic look out of his mind. He wrestled with images of Carolians tending crops under the watchful eyes of human masters. Then he thought about what he had heard at dinner earlier this evening.

Although it was not the red carpet treatment the Governor's meeting had portended, there had been a few of New California's movers and shakers at tonight's welcoming meal, among them Sacramento's Chief of Police and Mayor. Though the conversation had never really focused on Carolians, it had been filled with many off-color remarks about slugs, a pejorative slang used to describe *Cor Caroli's* native inhabitants. If he were ever going to make a connection with these creatures, it could not be in the company of his hosts. He had to get away from them. He had to show the Carolians that not all Earthmen were callous bigots.

Joshua lay on his back, watching the crocheted curtains fluttering in the breeze. His eyes adjusted to the night. The full moon, shining through the window, washed his room in a bright bluish glow. He could still hear the chants, but he'd begun to think that what he'd taken to be instruments might be something else. It was a strange sound, percussive perhaps, but with a hollow resonance of something he'd heard before in the course of his studies.

He was an anthropologist, steeped in the Earthly culture of the long past twentieth century. Joshua had always been fascinated by that time. It was a turning point in human societies, an explosion between two competing visions of the world. And it was also a time that had seen the beginning of the end of the ecosystem as it had been for thirty-thousand years of human history. By the end of the twenty-first century, most of the animal life on earth, excluding birds, insects, and people, had become extinct in the wild—because there was, for the most part, no wild left. But there were video and audio recordings of that time. The sound coming in the window right now bore an uncanny resemblance to the sound of frogs. He recognized the throaty hollow base of an impossible orchestra of bullfrogs, much like the four hundred year old recordings he had heard at the World Repository. But this chant wasn't the chaotic cacophony of amphibians in search of mates; it was more like organized music.

Joshua threw his covers aside and stepped to the window. He could still see the orange glow of the fire coming from somewhere far in the forest. Looking down, he noticed that the shingled roof sloped gently to a porch overhang no more than twelve feet off the ground. He remembered that thin columns—columns that he could easily shimmy down—supported the porch.

He got dressed, pocketed his camera and long distance audio ear, and slipped out the window. It was as easy as it had appeared. Before he knew it, he was on the lawn in front of the mansion and was jogging into the woods.

The night was magical. Though the forest was dense with trees, there wasn't much brush. He imagined the forest floor was much like that of conifer forests on old Earth. The ground was matted with layers of thin needle-like leaves that had fallen from the many trees. Apparently, the cover had kept the ground clear of hedges and briers. The tree trunks were thick and complex, like smooth wide stocks weaved together into a solid mass that rose high above the forest floor and exploded into a tangle of high branches. He had seen the trees in the daytime and knew they were rhubarb-red, but tonight they were indeterminately dark. Looking up, Joshua saw rays of moonshine beaming down in eerie columns that made ghostly spotlights on the forest floor from occasional breaks in the thick canopy. He hugged himself and felt goosebumps on his bare arms. It was cold. He'd forgotten to bring a sweater in his haste to leave the Governor's mansion.

Joshua stopped and looked around. Was he lost? He could still hear the music, but it was less distinct, more penetrating. It was no longer sharp and articulated. The baffling affect of the surroundings made it sound low and throbbing, like a heartbeat. He couldn't tell where it was coming from anymore. It was all around him. He stopped walking and took a breath, slowing panning three hundred and sixty degrees.

Two glowing eyes from somewhere above him were staring right at him. He'd forgotten that this wasn't Earth; animals weren't extinct. What kinds of animals were out in this forest? Could there be predators? Would the macho residents of New Sacramento allow predators this close to town? He took another breath. What the hell, Joshua thought, then continued his inspection of the surroundings, ignoring the watcher up in the trees. There was nothing he could do about the creature; he might as well stay calm—release as few pheromones as possible.

Then he saw it. There was a glow through the trees to his left. It was dim, but it looked like the fire he'd seen from his window. The fact that it was visible from this level meant it couldn't be that far away. Joshua started walking again, then quickened his pace to a jog.

The chanting got louder, and the glow got brighter. Joshua stepped from the forest into a clearing, and almost gasped when he saw it. Instead of the huts and makeshift shacks he'd expected, ahead of him stretched several complicated teepee shaped structures, some four or five stories high. They were made of smooth red wood, spiraling upward in a complicated construction of overlapping long panels to ornamental pinnacles. They had rock foundations, expertly set in perfect stacks with chiseled seams fitting together in complicated patterns.

Joshua approached the nearest structure and hesitantly put his hand on the smooth rock wall. It was cool and dry. He ran his hand along the wall until he came to a window. It was framed in wood with perfect glass panes set in red wood ribs. He looked up and saw the moonlight shining off the teepee as it rose high into the night.

Animals, Joshua thought. That's how Azise had described the Carolians—animals. He shook his head and followed a stone walkway further into the Carolian village. Why hadn't he seen these buildings from town? It must be that they were so well matched to the forest, that from a distance, they were indistinguishable. Up ahead were more buildings interspersed with trees, beyond which an orange light made everything seem to glimmer. Joshua was immersed in the strong throbbing chant. Though his body shook with each repetition, it did not hurt his ears because it was too low in frequency, more like a rumbling than a loud sound.

Finally, Joshua reached the center of town and the source of the chant. He crossed a circular stone street to a large plaza and found himself standing in front of a huge coliseum. Three levels of large stone arches loomed before him, one on top of the other. The whole structure must have been forty feet high, and three hundred feet across. The openings through the arches were ablaze in orange light. The top of the great structure was open, and a steady glow shown onto the low clouds that hung over the town.

Joshua was in awe, and completely confused. Nothing was as it seemed on *Cor Caroli*. Up till now, he had assumed than the natives were little more than a Bronze Age people who had been enslaved by the settlers. But this town showed an appreciation for geometric design that was, in some ways, more advanced than many human communities, and certainly more elegant than New Sacramento.

He made his way to one of the arches and peered into the coliseum. It descended in concentric stone steps like an amphitheater to a central platform. Carolians were seated on the steps, all gazing at a hemisphere in the middle of the platform, which was at least fifty feet below the first tier where he stood. The hemisphere seemed to be made of a clear stone, and was perfectly smooth. An intense orange glow emanated from the object and filled the amphitheater with light. The light was somehow focused by the structure and was shining into the sky like a searchlight. The extraordinary thing about it was that it didn't hurt his eyes. The light was incredibly bright, but, for some reason, Joshua was able to stare straight into it without even squinting. He noticed that the sound, as well, was being focused by the structure. This was truly an engineering marvel.

Captivated, Joshua slipped through the arch and sat on the uppermost step. He was completely swept up in the spectacle and no longer felt cold, or thirsty, or anything else. He just sat there, entranced by the light, swaying in the resonance of the chant.

Suddenly, Joshua sensed someone behind him. He turned quickly and flinched at the sight of a Carolian looking down at him. The creature's flat face seemed to float in the night, glowing in the orange light of the central stone.

"Come, sir," the creature said.

Joshua hesitated, then got to his feet and followed the Carolian into the plaza. He noticed that this Carolian was dressed in pants and a shirt, the same garb as his driver from the spaceport this afternoon. The Carolians he'd seen in the coliseum had been dressed in colorful robes that appeared, in the orange light, to be made of a course silk.

"Onda?" Joshua asked.

"Come, sir," the creature said, and started walking into the village.

Joshua followed a couple of steps behind. They wound through town on a footpath that snaked away from the plaza. Onda didn't say another word, nor did he bother looking to see if Joshua was still following. He simply continued toward the outskirts of the village in a steady kangaroo walk, using his tail as a third leg. Eventually, they came to one of the tee-pees. Onda stopped at the door and turned to Joshua. "Come in, sir," he said, then turned and slid the door open.

The inside of the structure was as impressive as its exterior. Joshua stood on a hardwood floor that was stained to resemble dark cherry. Panels, which threw no heat, rendered the interior of the dwelling in a warm and shadowless light, indistinguishable from daylight. Once the door was closed, he was enveloped in a deep silence; not a trace of the chant could be heard.

In the middle of the large room was a low table, around which were arranged large colorful pillows, much like the dinning areas of Japanese dwellings, which Joshua had seen at the World Repository.

"Please sit, sir," Onda said.

Once Joshua had settled on a pillow, Onda sat down across from him.

"Why have you come to the village, sir?" Onda asked.

"I wish to study your culture. That's why I'm here. I came a long way to understand your people. On Earth, I'm known as an anthropologist. It's my job to study other cultures."

Onda sat there, stoic. After a few moments, he said, "Why?"

Joshua didn't know what to say.

"Other Earthmen are not interested in our ways. They hate us, except for what we can do for them."

"You must believe me," Joshua said. "What these Earthmen have done is considered a crime on Earth."

"Why have other Earthmen not stopped them?" Onda asked.

Joshua exhaled. "Do you understand about the stars—the lights in the sky at night?"

Onda contorted his face into the wry look that Joshua had seen back at the Governor's mansion. "Yes, we understand the stars."

"Then you must know how far away they are. Other Earthmen on Earth don't know what the settlers have done here."

"And you will tell them?" Onda asked.

"Yes."

"Then you are in danger, Bernstein. You do not know your people the way we do. They will try to stop you, and they will harm you if they must."

Joshua considered this. He was not used to physical violence. He was an academic. The idea, as obvious as it was, had never occurred to him. "Yes," he said slowly. "Have the settlers ever harmed you—physically, I mean?"

"In the beginning, when you first came from the sky, Carolians greeted you as explorers. We helped you build the Earthman town. We showed you how to grow eina; you call wheat. At first, you were nice, but as you became stronger, you became cruel."

Joshua stared at Onda. He didn't know what to say. He felt ashamed, powerless.

"Your people have killed Carolians when we refused to continue work. We ask our god to send you away."

"The chant," Joshua said.

"Yes," Onda said.

Joshua put his face in his hands, then looked up. "They will be punished," he said.

"Yes," Onda said, then he got up and left the room.

Joshua sat in silence. What could he do? He looked around—Virginia. He would have to get in touch with the ship before it left. But in order to do that, he needed a transmitter, and the only transmitter was back in Sacramento. He exhaled.

Onda returned, carrying something. He put two cups on the table and poured from a beautifully ornate porcelain pitcher. "Drink, Bernstein," he said, then pushed the cup in front of Joshua.

Joshua raised the cup in both hands, breathing in the rich vapors. He took a sip, then blinked. "Why this is delicious. What is it?"

"Tea," Onda said.

Joshua sipped his tea, then put the cup down. "I'm going to call the ship—the craft in the sky that brought me. I will inform the authorities about the situation down here."

"You have a device to talk to other Earthmen, Bernstein?"

"No, but. . ."

"The gods will take Earthmen away," Onda interrupted.

Joshua searched for something reassuring, but he could think of nothing else to say. When they had finished their tea, Onda guided him back to the Governor's mansion in silence.

* * *

The next day Azise took him to a plain two-story brick building on the outskirts of Sacramento. Joshua was sandwiched between two large men in the rear seat of the car, with Onda at the wheel once more. As they drove, Joshua noticed the Carolian watching him in a small rectangular mirror that was suspended above the console of the ancient vehicle. When they finally arrived at their destination, Onda opened the rear door and Joshua stepped onto a hot asphalt street. The air was damp and full of the kind of fragrance only the presence of life could impart. The feeling of being on a planet again was intoxicating. Joshua paused a moment, enjoying the feel of solid ground beneath his feet. He sighed, then moved to join the others. They were waiting in front of a metal door in the shade of a mezzanine above the front entrance of the building. As he passed, he heard Onda whisper, "Be careful. Say nothing of our conversation."

Joshua hesitated, not daring to look at the Carolian, then walked on.

Once inside, Joshua was introduced to a small wiry man wearing a starched white coat.

"This is Dr. Marcum," Azise said.

The small man regarded Joshua wearily, then took off his gold-rimmed glasses and nervously polished them on his coat. Without his glasses, the man's round face, and the sparse strands of wispy fuzz on his receding hairline, made Joshua think of a turtle cautiously peeking out of its shell.

"Dr. Marcum has been examining the Artifact," Azise said.

Marcum nodded, glanced nervously at the two brawny men flanking Azise, and with an unsteady hand replaced the glasses on his beaky nose. Azise motioned with a sweep of his arm, "This way, Mista Bernstein."

The thing they called the Artifact was a black cylinder about two feet long and six inches wide. Stainless steel clamps, gleaming under bright lights, held it vertically in what looked like a glass-walled pressure chamber.

"We put it in vacuum because it makes loud noises when we probe it with microwaves," Marcum explained in a scratchy voice.

Joshua could see symbols etched into its dull onyx finish. He walked around the containment, trying to get a better look at the symbols that were cut all the way around as well as down its major axis.

"This is definitely a variation of Carolian," Joshua remarked excitedly.

"How do you know that?" Marcum asked, annoyed.

"I've been studying Carolian for many years now. It's my life's work; that's why I came here," Joshua said.

Marcum was looking at Azise, whose massive arms were folded across his chest below a stone cold face. The other two men were stationed at the door as if guarding something.

Joshua turned from the Artifact. In his excitement, he had failed to notice how tense his hosts were.

"What's going on here? Why all the security?" Joshua asked. When Azise failed to answer, Joshua said, "Just what is it you want from me, Governor?"

Azise walked over to the containment, staring straight ahead, not looking at Joshua. "I want you to tell me what this thing is," he growled. "And I want you to stop talking to the slugs."

He turned and glared down at Joshua, his deep brown eyes sinister and bloodshot. "Ever since we found that thing, the slugs have been gathering at night and singing those damned chants. They're refusing to work. A couple of farms in the south have had organized revolts." He turned back to the cylinder, staring at it with palpable hatred.

Joshua couldn't believe what he was hearing. Before he could stop himself, he blurted, "You know what you're doing here is illegal—and not only that, it's immoral. Your settlement was never sanctioned to come here and enslave these people."

"People," Azise hissed, his huge face flushed red hot with rage. What had been the rugged good looks of a pioneer settler twisted into a hate-filled mask of brutal blunt features. "These aren't people, they're animals—aliens. They're nothing compared to people." Azise spat a bitter laugh that gave Joshua the chills. "We came here from heaven," Azise declared. "That's what they said when we arrived—descended from the clouds like angels."

Azise stood menacingly close to Joshua, who could smell his pungent perspiration just under the sickly sweet scent of deodorant. Azise was no longer the friendly unassuming man who had met them at the shuttle landing. Over the past day, he had slowly metamorphosed into someone clearly unbalanced, perhaps even dangerous, Joshua thought.

Azise glanced back at the two men standing watch at the door. His eyelids were drawn, rendering his eyes little more than slits cut into a numb soulless face. In a low voice, he sneered, "Get him the hell outa here."

The two hulking men brushed past Marcum, almost knocking him down, and grabbed Joshua roughly. They then hustled him out of the building, past a shaken Marcum, onto the muggy street, then into the back seat of the car without a word.

"Drive tu-da brambles," one of the men ordered.

Onda hesitated. Joshua could see the Carolian's expressionless gray eyes staring at him in the rear view mirror.

"Damn it—get goin'," one of the men snapped.

At that the Carolian jerked something on the floor beside his seat, and the car pulled away from the curb with a teeth-grinding screech.

Soon Joshua found himself in a clearing in the middle of a large fern grove, somewhere in the jungle beyond the town. With one man on each arm, Joshua was dragged over rocks and sharp roots that protruded from the leaf-strewn ground. Briers tore his pants legs and dug painfully into his flesh. Joshua could taste his fear in the sour bile that rose into his mouth and mixed with the suffocating odors of the jungle.

They dumped him on the ground. When he tried to stand, one of the men kicked him in the stomach. Hot pain and nausea coursed through Joshua and he fell back. Then the beating started in earnest. They pummeled him with fists and feet. Joshua flailed under the blows like a rag doll being ravaged by a large dog. Eventually, his body went numb. He felt distant, as if the beating were happening to someone else. He was losing consciousness and feared he'd never wake up. They were going to kill him; he was sure of it.

One of the men kicked him again. Joshua landed on his back. Through blurry eyes, he noticed someone coming up fast behind his attacker. Whoever it was struck the man in the back of the head. He lurched forward, and went down hard. Then Joshua saw Onda bending over him and reaching down. But before the Carolian was able to prop him up, the other man came up behind Onda.

"Watch out," Joshua gurgled through the blood and saliva that pooled in his mouth—but he was too late. As if in slow motion, Joshua saw the man raise something resembling a rifle butt high into the gray sky above Onda's head. Then, in a swift deliberate arc, he hit Onda with a dull thud. The Carolian went down on top of him with crushing weight, knocking what little air was left in his lungs out of him. As Joshua struggled to remain conscious, he could hear sticks breaking and leaves rustling under the other man's hurried retreat. Unable to hold on any longer, Joshua registered distant footfalls echoing in his ears. They grew dimmer as he surrendered to an inky dreamless black.

* * *

Joshua pushed against whatever was holding him down. Suddenly, there were fists and feet again, and he reflexively wanted to reach up and cover his face—but something was stopping him.

"Easy, easy, Mr. Bernstein; it's alright."

Joshua wanted to see, but something was sticking his eyelids together. He struggled to open his eyes, and finally, with continued effort, he felt the crust starting to crumble, like crud flaking off an old jar lid. There was someone standing above him. Brown hands cuffed his wrists and pinned his arms to his chest in a suffocating embrace.

He remembered. The sons-of-bitches were trying to kill him. Panic shot through him, and he railed, pushing up with all his might.

"Get off me, you bastards!" Joshua yelled, as he squirmed and pushed with renewed vigor.

"Stop it!" came a brisk report.

He stopped in mid squirm, blinking, trying to clear his vision, trying to see. Slowly, there was a face. Its soft smooth lines were somehow familiar, yet different. Above the dark young face of an attractive woman shone something white—a halo. Joshua smiled, almost laughed out loud.

"I'm dead—right? And you're what, an angel?" He laughed at the sound of the words, then stopped, gazing into the deep brown almond eyes.

"Virginia?"

"Yes, Mr. Bernstein. How do you feel?"

He felt her loosen his wrists. He tried to rise, then had to contend with a bout of vertigo. Lying back down seemed very attractive.

Virginia placed a firm open hand on his back and helped him into a sitting position. A scaly four-fingered hand held a cup of something to his lips.

"Drink—" came the guttural tone of a Carolian.

Onda pressed the water to his lips and Joshua drank. The cool water hurt all the way down at first, but after a few moments Joshua drank greedily. He felt his strength returning, just before all the aches and pains hit with a vengeance.

"Oh shit," Joshua moaned.

Virginia smiled.

He closed his eyes and smiled back. "What happened to you, too much sun?" He laughed again, but caught himself when the pain in his ribs protested the expansion of his chest, causing him to issue a couple of dry hacks.

"We have a situation," Virginia remarked.

"A situation?"

"Yes, can you stand? We have to go to the Governor's mansion."

"The Governor?" Joshua scoffed. "The man's a criminal." He looked up at Onda. "Azise is a criminal," Joshua repeated.

Onda looked back at him with the characteristic vacant stare that Joshua was starting to find strangely endearing.

"Yes, I can travel," Joshua said, rising on rubbery legs. Virginia's strong hand braced his right forearm and Joshua settled in a shaky stance.

Soon they emerged, in hazy sunlight, into the stone streets of the Carolian village.

"I will go ahead," Onda declared.

When Virginia nodded, Onda sprang, hopping away at a blazing speed toward a grove of large wine-colored trees at the border of the village.

Joshua couldn't help smiling. When Virginia glanced at him, eyebrows arched, he said, "I've always thought of them as slow."

"This way, Mr. Bernstein," Virginia said, then started toward the same trees into which Onda had just disappeared.

Carolians dressed in green, blue, and wine-red muslin robes collected in small groups in the street and stared at the aliens. Joshua stared too. Virginia, in a form-fitting silver shipboard jumpsuit, was a dark coffee brown under a shock of platinum hair. She stopped in the middle of the dusty street amid a group of Carolians, who were regarding her with the same admiring deference, and turned to Joshua.

"Well?"

"Yes," Joshua said.

"Are you coming, Mr. Bernstein?"

"Yes, of course."

Joshua followed her into the trees. "How did you get so dark?" Joshua asked.

"I can control my skin tone." She looked toward the sun. "Being darker is beneficial under the ultraviolet rays of the star."

"You're a chameleon."

Virginia smiled, then led him to a clearing among the trees. Onda was waiting next to a dull gray platform that stood a foot above the forest floor on four shiny silver struts. Virginia stepped onto the thing and gestured for him and Onda to climb aboard. Onda jumped up, slowly straightened, then stood next to Virginia. Once Joshua had joined them, a circular railing appeared from the perimeter of the disk and silently rose midway to the level of Joshua's chest. After each of them grabbed the railing, Joshua heard a hissing noise, like steam from a pipe, and the platform rose smoothly above the trees. It pitched forward a few degrees, then sped above the forest toward town.

Joshua couldn't help laughing out loud against the rushing wind that brushed his face as they weaved and bobbed above the dark green fabric of the forest. Even Onda seemed to be smiling with delight at this unexpected turn of events. But none of their pleasure was reflected in Virginia's stern eyes, which seemed out of place both with their avian freedom, and with her otherwise optimistic manner.

Joshua put his hand over hers. He was reminded of their strange communion aboard the *Hera*, which had never strayed far from his thoughts since coming to *Cor Caroli*. "Come on, lighten up," Joshua said, smiling as she turned to look at him.

Just then, there was a tremendous flash and Joshua saw the forest replaced by a black and white animationscape reminiscent of a colorless photograph. He squeezed his eyes shut, and heard Onda issue a pained wail. The platform shuttered as though hit by a shockwave. He tightened his grip on the railing and on Virginia's hand. He felt the platform bank, precess slowly, and then right itself into a hover.

"What the hell was that?" Joshua said.

Virginia was rubbing her eyes; Onda was gazing upward with a strange look on his scaly face, his large gray eyes trained on a spot in the hazy sky.

"The gods have returned," the Carolian whispered. Then looking directly at Joshua, "Our gods have returned, as they promised. We left their scepter for the Earthmen to find, as they instructed us. We knew that the Earthmen would violate it with their machines and summon our gods."

"The scepter?" Virginia asked.

"He means the Artifact," Joshua said.

Virginia regarded him with a quizzical stare.

"Azise and some farmers found a cylinder buried on a farm somewhere on the outskirts of town. Apparently, the object is of alien origin." Joshua had to smile at the obvious contradiction. "They wanted me to interpret the writing on the thing; I think it's a form of Carolian."

"What did it say?" Virginia asked evenly.

"Don't know. Azise and his goons got angry about my sympathizing with the Carolians. They took me out and had me beaten before I had a chance to translate it." Joshua thought a moment, "By the way, how'd you find me?"

"You're my charge," Virginia said.

"Your charge?"

"Yes, my charge. We were entangled, you and I. Don't you remember?"

Before Joshua could respond, Onda said, "There is stirring in the Earthman town."

Joshua and Virginia followed Onda's downward gaze. They were hovering over Main Street, near the Governor's mansion. Below, humans and Carolians had gathered in the street in front of the garish cream-colored building with its black slatted shutters, which, to Joshua, harkened back to images of colonial times he'd encountered in his studies. Armed men were pushing the crowd of Carolians away from the mansion as townspeople hurdled racial epithets and catcalls at the hapless natives.

"Oh for Christ sake," Joshua said at the sight of his fellow humans harsh behavior. He glanced at Virginia, then at Onda. "We humans don't travel well—I'm sorry."

"As am I," Onda said.

They descended into the street between the armed settlers and the retreating crowd of Carolians in a cloud of dust and vapor. The shouts of men and women as well as the panicked singsong wails of Carolians were drowned out by the rising whine of the sky platform's engines as it came to rest smoothly on the ground. It abruptly shut down, leaving an eerie silence. As the railing smoothly lowered into the body of the gray disk and vanished, crowds on either side of the platform looked on in stunned silence, not knowing quite what to do.

Virginia stepped into the asphalt street and took a couple of steps toward the settlers, stopping in front of a large squared-jawed man, his rifle muzzle a couple of inches from her chest. The man was sweating profusely; large dark stains shadowed his armpits, and his red eyes twitched as sweat dripped into them.

"No—please don't shoot her," Joshua cried. He jumped into the street and ran up behind Virginia. She caught him with a hand, holding him back, never taking her dark eyes off the man. With her other hand, she slowly reached out, cupped the top of the rifle barrel, and pushed it down until it was pointing at the street. The man's heavily muscled arms just let it fall, his eyes darting from Virginia to the platform and back again. He slowly turned his head, as if beseeching his fellow settlers to help him.

"I want you all to go home now," Virginia said simply. "You people." She looked beyond the man. "That's enough now; I want you all to go home."

A rifle lowered, followed by another, and so on, until all of them were pointing at the ground. People in the crowd looked around blankly, as if they'd been sleepwalking and suddenly woke up to find themselves in the middle of the street. They didn't seem to have the slightest clue why they were there. The crowd slowly dispersed; people broke into small groups and began slipping away. The man turned back to Virginia, looking a little calmer now. As Joshua looked on in amazement, she moved the hand that cupped the rifle barrel, reached up, and soothingly wiped the sweat from his eyes.

"Go home," she said softly. He turned and walked away.

"What in the world just happened?" Joshua asked. "I thought he was going to kill you. What did you do to him?"

"Let's go inside, Mr. Bernstein."

She turned and started for the mansion. Joshua stood in the middle of the humid sun-bleached street, watching as she mounted the stairs to the mansion, sparkling in her silver suit. Onda followed, using his thick tail to cantilever up the stairs behind her. Joshua realized he'd been holding his breath, exhaled, shook his head, and fell in behind them.

Virginia pushed the large wooden door open at the top of the mansion's grand entrance and disappeared into the dark cavernous shadow of its interior. Joshua followed Onda inside. He heard the big wooden door slam shut behind him, and was immediately blinded by the ensuing darkness. He stood there, waiting for his eyes to adjust.

The mansion's ornate interior slowly began materializing from the cool dark veil of the room. Joshua caught movement and noticed Onda slipping out of sight, turning into a corridor on the far side of the large circular foyer. He hurried across the cherry and blonde parquet floor, under a grand crystal chandelier, and ran into a long plaster corridor with oil paintings adorning its walls in carved baroque frames. When he finally caught up with Onda and Virginia, he found them once again in a face-off, this time with a couple of heavily-armed men guarding an elevator. Both men's eyes were glued to Onda with that palpable mixture of hatred and disgust that he'd grown wearily used to during his brief time on this unfortunate planet. Like on the street outside, the men lowered their arms and stepped absently aside under Virginia's inscrutable prompting. The more he knew her, the less he understood who she really was. She had power that was mysterious and frightening, but at the same time, in the hands of someone of such unshakable integrity, indispensable and welcome.

They rode the elevator to the Governor's suite on the third floor. An anticipatory silence had Joshua wondering whether he'd escaped assassination only to find his way back so that Azise could finish the job properly this time. As expected, they encountered more guards on the way to Azise's office, but like on the first floor, Virginia's mysterious hypnotic prompting dispatched them too.

Joshua followed Virginia through large wooden double doors into Azise's inner sanctum.

* * *

"Bernstein!" Harris exclaimed. "The Governor just told us that you'd been mortally injured in an accident."

"An accident of his own making," Joshua said.

"Mr. Azise, is this true?" Harris asked.

"Shut up and sit down," Azise growled. "How convenient that you should come back, Bernstein—saves us the trouble of finding you."

It was like old home week. Harris was standing there staring at the Governor, who was sitting in a large leather chair behind an enormous light brown wooden desk. Mugabe sat next to Irene on a black leather sofa on the other side of the room, and Marcum was standing near the sofa, forever wiping his glasses on his suit coat. The two men who had beaten the crap out of him earlier were there too, armed and standing to the left of the door.

"Mr. Azise," Virginia said. "You are in clear violation of a large number of settlement laws. I'm going to have to ask you to step down. A suitable court will be convened, charges formulated, and a determination will be made as to who else is responsible here."

Azise laughed out loud. "Now look here missy, you may make some people nervous in that silly silver suit, but I don't think you're in any position to demand anything."

"The *Hera* is a powerful ship," Harris said.

"Maybe for jumping around from star to star, yes," Azise said mockingly. "But as far as the use of force against settlers, I don't think so."

Virginia started forward.

"Take her into custody," Azise demanded.

This time, to Joshua's horror, Virginia was grabbed by one of the large men and held firmly by the arm. She did not resist.

"Make him back down," Joshua cried. "Like you did before."

But Virginia let herself be handled roughly. She was made to stand aside. Azise laughed again, the savage guttural laugh of a deranged little boy. Then he turned his attention to Onda.

"A slug in my office," Azise said slowly, like the calm preamble to a looming storm. "Take it out and shoot it—not here, of course. I don't want his purple blood staining my carpet." Then Azise laughed again.

"Run Onda," Joshua shouted, remembering how fast Onda was.

But Onda just stood there, even more passive than usual.

Joshua turned to Virginia. "For God's sake, do something."

"Come on now," Azise said. "Get him outa here."

One of the men descended on Onda, trying to grab him by the shoulders and turn him around. But as soon as the man touched him, his hands exploded in a blue crackle of sparks that turned the room incandescent. Smoke rose from every exposed surface on the man's body as he shook and danced a spastic jitter in the corona of blue electricity. Finally, the crackling stopped and he crumpled to the floor. The sickening smell of burnt flesh hung heavy in the room. Everyone just stared wide-eyed at Onda.

"May I?" Virginia asked.

Onda nodded, and Virginia stepped forward and placed a small gray disk on Azise's expansive desk. The Governor looked on, his mouth agape, shifting his eyes from the smoking huddled form of the man's body on the floor to Virginia.

"What's the matter, Governor, afraid he'll stain your fucking rug with his burnt flesh?" Harris gibed.

Suddenly, the top of the disk glowed amber. A stunning holographic image of *Cor Caroli Alpha Four* materialized in vivid splotchy greens and reds partially obscured by circular wisps of white clouds in the space above the Governor's desk. Above the slowly rotating planet, the immense bronze disk of the *Hera* held station five hundred miles above New California. Off in a far corner of the room, *Cor Caroli Alpha Four's* moon hung in space, its bluish crescent shining bright.

No sooner had Joshua noticed it, than a bright flash of light pierced every corner of the room, then just as quickly vanished.

"This is an image taken by observation satellites dispatched from *Hera* a half hour ago," Virginia said.

"How did you know? You're down here with us," Joshua said.

Virginia smiled at him. "Implants, Mr. Bernstein."

"Of course," Joshua said. "How silly of me."

Still smiling, Virginia continued. "Notice the object now holding station behind the moon."

As everyone in the room strained to see, a pulsating golden sphere moved from behind the moon, and with blinding speed, moved past *Hera* and settled two hundred miles above the town, which was marked by a flashing red dot on the planet's surface.

"What is it?" Harris asked.

"I'm not sure exactly," Virginia admitted. "But I think the flash was the object shunting a large amount of energy after materializing from a tunnel and emerging into normal space at a dead stop. Something, I might add, that is far beyond our technology. Apparently, the object used the moon to eclipse its energy wake so as not to harm life on the planet, a feat of navigation that is also far beyond our capabilities."

"What's going on here?" Azise whimpered.

"I don't know, why don't you ask him?" Virginia said, glancing at Onda.

"The slug?" Azise asked, bewildered. "What would he know bout such things?"

"That's not Onda," Virginia said. Then looking over at Joshua, anticipating his question, she said, "I can see in the infrared. As soon as he entered the room, I noticed Onda's body temperature had risen beyond what his metabolism can support."

Onda stepped forward, brushing by the charred hulk of the man on the floor. He stood above a cowering Azise. "If you threaten danger, you will be the object of danger," Onda said in clear colloquial English.

"Who are you?" Virginia asked.

Onda didn't take his eyes off Azise, who continued sinking further into his chair, no longer an imposing figure now that he'd lost the upper hand.

"We are the Collective."

"The Collective," Joshua said. "Are you the gods of the Carolians? Was it your scepter that the settlers found?"

Onda turned from Azise. "Ah, Mr. Bernstein. Your people, the humans of the Blue Planet, owe you a debt of thanks."

"Me?" Joshua asked. "Why me, I know very little about all this."

"You know more than you think. You know how to conduct yourself in a civilized manner. You know how to show kindness and respect to strangers. The beings you call Carolians are our incarnation in this stunted dimensional universe of yours. And yes, it was our, their, scepter you found."

Joshua was frustrated. He wanted to understand, but didn't know enough, was woefully unfamiliar with the terms Onda was using. He looked to Virginia for help; she, unlike him, understood the subtleties of the physical universe.

"Stunted dimensions," Virginia said. "Are you from a greater dimensional manifold in which our three-dimensional hyperplane is embedded?"

"Yes," Onda said simply.

"What does that mean?" Joshua asked, still hopelessly in the dark.

"We have long thought that the universe was constructed from more than three spacial dimensions," Virginia said. "Elegant theories, but as of this time, we've been unable— haven't had the resources to confirm the conjecture."

Joshua struggled to understand. "But if there are higher dimensions, why can't we experience them?"

Onda said, "There is a precipitate that permeates your three-dimensional hyperplane. It anchors you here by construction. Few influences that you know of are free of the precipitate; our scepter employs such an influence. You call it gravity."

"Precipitate?" Joshua said. Every new thing that Onda described was more confusing and cryptic than the last.

"You mean the Higgs field?" Virginia asked.

There was a sound that made Joshua think of soft laughter. "Yes, Higgs field." Onda laughed again. "Gravity is only partially anchored by the Higgs field. Its influence seeps away into the higher dimensions where we can hear it." Onda stepped toward Virginia. "We saw your craft, the disk, skimming above the hyperplane of your universe, then heard the call of our scepter. Our scepter was only made to call if something harmful was infecting our representatives here." Onda turned to Azise. "Something virulent and corrosive."

"We assumed that your craft was the infectious agent and were going to destroy it. But when we integrated into this space, we were given a greater appreciation of the situation by Onda's communion with Mr. Bernstein. We choose to reserve judgment."

"Why are you here?" Virginia asked. "Why recreate yourselves to live in this stunted universe at all? And why are your representatives here without technology? Yours is obviously a tremendously advanced civilization, but the Carolians are simple tribal people."

"We are explorers," Onda said. "We wish to know what it's like to be in a room, like this one." He looked around in amazement, then looked back at Virginia. "To think that we are actually contained by its six simple walls. We wish to experience the linear sequencing of events in what you call cause and effect—a charming concept."

There was a joy in Onda's voice that was not reflected in his stoic face—a solemn face without the plastic flexibility of its human counterpart.

"Our representatives here, the Carolians as you call them, are to us what your sense organs are to you. They give us the experience of sight, touch, smell, and other senses in a universe that is intrinsically separate from ours. Why employ technology if none is needed? Do your fingers, nose, or ears require technology for you to experience the world? Before you humans came from the Blue Planet, our representative's sojourn on this orb was pleasant and rich with natural experience.

"The Carolians are your representatives?" Virginia asked. "What does that mean?"

Onda stared at her. "Yes, perhaps you can understand. The universe is a hierarchy of dimensional realms. But these realms are not separate; they are dependent on one another."

"Dependent—how?" Virginia asked.

"Your universe is a representation of the boundary layer of a lesser universe. All that you perceive and experience is a projection of that universe, which has only two extended spatial dimensions. You would see this universe as a true two-dimensional surface, but it creates your universe as a two-dimensional hologram creates a three-dimensional image. Our universe is higher in dimensionality than yours, so to us, you inhabit a surface.

Joshua was dumfounded. He now understood less than before Onda's explanation. Though he didn't understand the techie mumbo-jumbo, he did intuit the point—at least he thought he did. "Are you saying that somehow the Carolians are some kind of inverse projection of you—that the Carolians are not your *representatives*, but your *representation*?"

"Yes of course, Mr. Bernstein. You do understand," Onda said.

Joshua saw that Virginia was smiling. He shrugged.

"We were pleased with this rich environment," Onda mused. "Then you came." Onda turned swiftly on Azise, who appeared pale and shrunken. "You came with your senseless cruelty and greed. When we first learned of you, we anticipated a mutually beneficial meeting of explorers. But after hearing the call of the scepter, we soon learned of your willful crimes against us. We are not without anger."

"We can withdraw our people," Virginia said. "Will that be sufficient to quell your rightful anger?"

Onda turned to Virginia, blinked for the first time, and said, "Yes, Pilot. Take your brethren and leave our people in peace."

Joshua felt a crushing sadness. He had come to live among the only other sentient beings that humanity had ever found, and now, within reach of cultural riches beyond his wildest dreams, it was all slipping away.

"Wait," Joshua said. "I want to stay. I'm an explorer too. I have lost my place in time and space. I will never return to the Earth I left. I came here to live among Carolians. It's been my life's work."

"If your brethren agree, perhaps you can make an exception of Mr. Bernstein," Virginia said.

Onda turned to Joshua. "Yes. Perhaps in the case of Mr. Bernstein."

"Also," Virginia said. "The *Hera* is not big enough to evacuate the entire human population all at once. It will take a hundred standard Earth years to completely leave *Cor Caroli*. Can you trust us to keep our word?"

"We can help you in this," Onda said. "We can transport your people."

Virginia's eyebrows arched. "You can transport fifty thousand people one hundred and thirty light years—safely? How long will it take?"

"They can be on the Blue Planet when we leave, as you measure time. For them, it will be the time of their original departure from the Blue Planet, at least for those who were not conceived here on Twie-Twie-Tononga."

Virginia stared at Onda. "Such things are possible?"

"Yes, Pilot, such things are indeed possible."

Joshua was struck by the fact that even Virginia seemed awed by the almost god-like accomplishments of what at first had appeared a simple tribal people. He remembered Carolians hopping about the rows of wheat under straw hats, below a golden valley sun, in the shadow of azure mountains.

Onda leaned forward precariously, teetering as if he were going to fall. Joshua caught him by the arm. Harris grabbed his other arm, and they helped him to the sofa. Marcum and Irene got up as they approached. The hologram, still present above the room, must have been playing in real time now. Stooping next to Onda, Joshua watched as the pulsating sphere seemed to light up, streak past the *Hera* suspended over their heads, and disappear into the star-laden space beyond.

"The gods have left?" Onda whispered in his characteristic rasp.

"But what about our people?" Joshua asked. "They said they were going to take them back to Earth?"

"*Hera* reports that the entire human population of *Cor Caroli Alpha Four* now consists of twenty-five human biosignatures," Virginia said.

Joshua turned to Onda, "But how?"

"Of what do you speak?" Onda asked. "The Earthmen are gone? Have the gods taken them away?"

"He doesn't remember," Joshua said.

"No," Virginia said. "And it is not for us to disturb the intentions of the Collective."

"Of what does the Pilot speak?" Onda asked, trying to sit up.

"As usual, I haven't the slightest idea," Joshua said.

* * *

Joshua stood on the tarmac beneath the massive bronze profile of the shuttle, its underbelly scorched black by the many flaming reentries into planetary atmospheres.

"Azise and his associates will be placed in stasis and surrendered to the authorities on our return to Earth," Virginia said.

The twenty-five remaining settlers—including Azise and his collaborators, the ones that the Collective felt were most responsible for the mistreatment of their representatives—had been left in Virginia's custody. Humans were expected to deal with their own demons, in whatever way they saw fit. Apparently, after the standoff in Azise's office, there had been no further conditions imposed by the Collective on the offending humans, other than they leave *Cor Caroli*.

"Let's not talk about them. I want to forget them," Joshua said. Then, after a moment's reflection, "You were right, you know. I won't be going back. How did you know this was going to be a one-way ticket for me?"

After regarding him for several long moments, Virginia said, "Don't forget me, Mr. Bernstein."

"How could I ever do that; we're entangled you and I, don't you remember?"

Virginia cocked her head in that way she did, and smiled. "I have some things for you, Joshua."

Joshua raised his eyebrows; it was the first time she had ever addressed him by his first name. Behind her, on the asphalt, he noticed several gray molded plastic suitcases.

"An eternal battery, cyber-cube and display, orbital communications telephone, and ..."

"Thanks," Joshua interrupted. "Will I see you again, in the flesh, I mean?"

Catching him by surprise, Virginia came close, put her arms around him, and hugged him tight, pressing her head against his for a long while. She then released him and said, "Perhaps."

* * *

For a long time after she left, Joshua watched the place in the clouds where the shuttle had disappeared—long after the roar of the engines had subsided, long after the contrail had begun to smear, long after Virginia's strange but pleasant scent had faded. For some reason, he couldn't take his eyes off the spot. The air was warm and fragrant, full of the rich essence of alien flowering plants—and something else. A soft breeze felt fresh on his face and the world was quiet, except for the almost imperceptible rumble of an engine somewhere behind him.

"Your bags, sir"—the low voice of a Carolian.

"Yes, but I'll take them myself," Joshua said as he turned. He stuck his hand out and shook the four-fingered hand in a slow rhythmic sway. He knew Carolians did not like abrupt motions.

"Is this an Earthman custom?" the Carolian asked.

"Yes, I suppose it is."

"Will you be staying in the Earthman town, sir?"

"No, I'd rather stay in your village—that is, if you'll have me."

"There is space for you, sir. Onda has instructed me to bid you welcome to our town."

They walked to the SUV; Joshua, bags in hand, couldn't help smiling at that. And when his bags were loaded, they sped off, followed by a cloud of rust-brown dust, toward the distant blue mountains among golden rows of shimmering Carolian wheat.

The End

Four: The Dark before the End

"For the want of a nail the shoe was lost,
For the want of a shoe the horse was lost,
For the want of a horse the rider was lost,
For the want of a rider the battle was lost,
For the want of a battle the kingdom was lost,
And all for the want of a horseshoe-nail."
— Benjamin Franklin

The Dark before the End

I feel the dark closing in on me, like some choking liquid, making its way into my lungs and forcing my chest to heave and my heart to race. Call it a premonition. They say that your life flashes before you at a time like this, but that's not what I'm seeing. No, instead, I'm standing in the make-shift dining room of our small vacation bungalow on the north shore of Kauai, thinking about the last half hour.

Dining room is a stretch. Actually, the whole house is little more than one big room that serves as a dining room, living room, and my personal den, depending on who's around at the time. At this particular moment, in my escapist daydream, I'm the only one left, and I've just gotten up from the table, my cereal still making that crackling sound in the milk. Something's happening outside, something expected, yet unbelievable. Like a zombie in some Kafkaesque dream, I rise and float to the large plate glass window that subtends the tropical beachscape beyond the house.

There's the sandy white beach just in front of the white picket fence that separates our grassy yard from the beach proper. But, unlike an hour ago, or yesterday, or all the yesterdays before that, there's no water. Instead, the beach slowly turns into a huge field of smooth small stones that gleam in the sun from the sheen of wetness that still coats their white, gray, and black surfaces. Farther out, I can see larger rocks inundated with rusty barnacles and seaweed, fol-lowed by long shelves of coral, jutting up like pitted hulks of ancient ships, except for their art deco colors that show a mother-of-pearl rainbow of hues. In the distance, the land drops off altogether like the impossible walls of a super

Grand Canyon that stretches into all I can see to the north and south. In the distant west, there's water, dull and unnaturally still, ominous under a hazy gunmetal gray sky. And, in the far distance to the west, where the gray water meets the gray sky, I see a strange band of black. It looks like the line that a child would draw into a picture with a black crayon.

I feel vertigo, nausea; I don't want to be here. I want this whole episode to be a dream, something born out of a bowl of bad chili. Then suddenly, as if my wish has come true, I'm no longer here. Instead, it's six months ago, and, as far as I know, all is right with the world.

It's funny how at any given time something can be happening in the world, something so causally disconnected from your life that you are mercifully spared any knowledge of it. It may be that in the vague tomorrows a train wreck is set into motion by obscure and coolly dispassionate forces. And, so it was for me, six blessed months ago as I streaked across the Pacific in a Navy Sea Stallion helicopter.

The world is flat in all directions; only the gray blue sea, punctuated by shining undulations, gives the panorama any texture. White billowing clouds loom in a robin's egg sky as the helicopter speeds into the vast seascape with no apparent destination.

I feel an elbow to my side and turn to see Ron Ashworthy, the Navy Lieutenant who met me in Guam as my escort. Ron points into the distance. As I follow his finger to the horizon, the helicopter banks sharply, as if on cue. I try to hold fast, but fall heavily against him.

"Sorry," I say into the microphone at my chin.

"Over there," says Ashworthy, a note of excitement creeping into his voice.

I strain my eyes to see what he's pointing at, but all I see are more of the same endless swells.

"Where?" I yell over the thudding of the blades.

Ron grabs my arm and, in a crouch, hustles me to the open door. I resist, but reluctantly let myself be led, not wanting to appear the novice. As he holds my arm in an iron grip, we both lean out of the Stallion's door, and Ron points emphatically toward the horizon in front of us.

"There," he yells.

In the distance, I think I see a black spot appear and disappear randomly in the roiling ocean.

"Oh yeah," I shout. "Yeah, I see it."

Ron glances at me, beaming a smile of blinding white teeth. I'm glad to be viewing the spectacle through sunglasses. I would say anything to keep Ron from leaning further out the door. When he nods in satisfaction, I slowly creep back into the helicopter and the safety of solid objects.

As we get closer, the single blemish in the infinite blue is no longer blinking in and out of sight, but starts to differentiate into a set of smaller black dots. It soon becomes apparent that we are closing in on a man-made island. We bank quickly and circle around, giving us a view of the aquatic city below. The black dots become a collection of huge oil platforms, bigger than anything I have ever seen floating. Each of them would dwarf the largest aircraft carrier. I can hear myself whistling into the microphone at the sight.

I start to count them. There are eight platforms arranged in an octagon surrounding a central circular hub, connected by an array of suspended monorails, like the spokes of an enormous wheel.

"What the hell is that?" I yell.

The wind blowing into the open door is so strong that both Ashworthy and I are magically prevented from falling forward, though we are both leaning towards the door. Ashworthy smiles.

"The drilling boom is over three hundred feet tall." He points to a latticework of long pipes piled onto rotating cylinders arranged like huge bleachers surrounding the central boom.

"That's the magma conduit," he yells.

I later learned that the borehole was more than six thousand feet below the platform, and three miles into the earth's crust.

When I felt the ground move a half hour ago, I knew what it was. I'm no longer in the helicopter, I'm here again, at the end of a long chain of dominos that I helped set into motion. It's still vivid in my minds' eye—the wary looks around the table as I delivered my final report.

"Drilling into the largest magma pocket ever discovered, close to the top of the earth's crust, promises hundreds of years of clean, free energy. And no, there will be no fractures, no cracks that can result in a rupture and subsequent earthquake," I assured.

As if awaiting a nightmare to finally arrive, I feel a strange relief that I no longer have to dread the dark, which even now slowly engulfs the front room. I know what it is. But like a reflex, I can't help racing to the large window. I have to crane my neck, look high to see the top of the black mass slowly covering the sky, turning day to night.

It's an impossibly dark featureless mountain whose scale renders it an abstraction more than something real. I feel calm, detached. It slowly rises out of the sea in defiance of all our planning. A mountain that I had assured Ashworthy and the rest of the drill team would never come, could never come. That's why I'm here, where the last domino should fall, to prove the point. Apparently, the joke's on me.

The sound is deafening, the whole house is shaking, falling down around me. All-of-a-sudden, it's cold to the bone and damp, like being underwater without being wet. I crumple under the suffocating pressure. I have the strange sense that I'm the last man on earth. It's completely black, I can't see a thing. I hear the window shatter above the roar of the wave—feel the immense force of the mountain of ice cold water a fraction of a second before I feel nothing at all.

The End

Author's Note

Special thanks to Jim Moose and Anne Moose for editing *Parallax*, and to Anne Moose for editing *End of the World* and *One Way Ticket*. Any errors that remain are my own.

About the Author

Peter Dingus is a physicist. He received his Ph.D. from UC Berkeley in 1988, and has had posts at *Ecole Polytechnique* in Paris, DESY in Hamburg, and CERN in Geneva. From 1991 until it was shut down in 1993, he was a staff physicist at the Superconducting Super Collider project, in Dallas, TX.

Dr. Dingus has published over fifty scientific papers in refereed journals (such as "Physical Review Letters"). In the mid-nineties, he left particle physics to work in the field of Speech Recognition. Since then, he has been a principal in two software startups and the co-founder of a third. He lives with his wife in Mission Viejo, California. Currently, he is CTO of a solar PV R&D company in Southern California.

www.ingramcontent.com/pod-product-compliance
Lightning Source LLC
Chambersburg PA
CBHW071945170626
46813CB00005B/1839